SOUL KILLER

SOUL JACKER 3

by Michael John Grist

ISBN: 9781097555604

THE COMPLETE **SOUL JACKER** TRILOGY

Soul Jacker (Book 1)

Soul Breaker (Book 2)

Soul Killer (Book 3)

See a full glossary of terms at the back of the book.

For Joe and Alice, my earliest chord.

CONTENTS

ME

--.

ME

1. HOLLOW DESERT

The Hollow Desert lies vast and golden around me.

I'm standing in a new body, one of the 'hands' cored by King Ruin to serve as his slaves, but still I'm Me, captain of the chord. I look out across the deep wilds of desert sand from my perch seven stories high at the forward prow of King Ruin's old suprarene, a massive building of a tank rumbling on great caterpillar treads.

It's early afternoon, and a glorious molten sun beats down on the endless waves of dunes from a plastic blue sky, making them shine like the promised land.

It's just another raid.

Tiny grains of sand skirl across the metal-grille gantry beneath my combat-booted feet, blown by a hot and rising wind. The railing under my fingers is warm and smooth, polished by the hands of countless arene commanders dating back to the earliest days of the War.

I notice these kinds of details now, when I know I'm going to die. It's strange. I notice that the sun is hot on my cheek, but a dry wind sucks away my sweat in seconds, something I can't get used to about the desert. I can't even sweat here. This body was made for the sand, but not me. I'm a sublavic marine, not a desert arene, and I belong in a ship deep within a Molten Core.

But here I am.

I look out toward the target. Beyond the undulating golden dunescape, studded with brownish-green outcroppings of cacti, lie a few pale tan escarpments of ancient rock rising in a spine-like ridge a few clicks distant. They could be shark fins on a solid ocean of sand. Between here and there are three villages hidden behind the vales of yellow, and beneath them, a Court.

It's a raid. It's a war. It's just another way to die.

The air smells of corroded metal and old salt.

"This is the life," I whisper to myself.

Ray snorts from behind me. "Cleaning up death camps is not my idea of fun."

I turn to him. He hasn't died since Becoming, hasn't had to, so he's still in the body of the first hand he took; a copper-skinned Darain dressed in full arene combat gear. He's leaning casually against the railing, picking at his teeth with a coil of gun spring, looking at me with his usual blend of cheerful insolence.

Of course, this is Ray. A year has passed since we Became true individuals in Ritry Goligh's world, but still it's strange to see him like this, without his glinting tooth-loops, without his pure black skin. Instead he's added a strange kind of fractal pattern tattoo across his left temple, which I know is a memento of Doe. Without Doe none of us would be alive.

The year since we buried her in the sand feels like a lifetime.

"I know what your idea of fun is," I say. "Is there anyone on this tank you haven't screwed?"

Ray laughs, rich and belly-deep. I laugh too. This is how it goes.

"Yena," comes So's voice from below, three decks down. She's in my head, like they all are now. There's no need for blood-mic when we're just facets of one Soul split across the aetheric bridge. "He wouldn't dare."

Ray nods. "She's right, Me, I wouldn't do that. Yena's all yours."

"Very kind."

Things have changed a lot since our Bathyscaphe days.

I know that Ray has been sleeping around so much because of Doe, because he misses her, and that's why I'll only gently tease him. I know how much it hurts him that she's gone, because it hurts me as well, and what harm is there in finding solace in lust? We're all addicted to something, now.

Far hardly ever leaves the aether, jacking deeper and further for days at a time, searching for something none of us understand. The twins, La and Ti, avoid each other compulsively. They've put thousands of kilometers between each other, as some kind of reaction to finding the freakish husk of King Ruin's twin. It was just too much, I suppose, to see twins like that. I think it's sad, but maybe they'll get over it.

So's addiction is building the map. She never really sleeps, only crashes out from exhaustion, refusing to take her eyes off it voluntarily except to use the bathroom, and even then she watches through the eyes of a borrowed hand.

And Me?

I die.

"We need to focus," I say. "So, give me what you've got."

We turn our thoughts to So, down in the suprarene's control cab on the sixth floor, working on readouts, dials and radar. I close my eyes on the blistering Hollow Desert and look out through her eyes to the holographic map hanging above the projection desk. Circling it are three techs; she knows their names but I don't, which is what the hierarchy of command is for.

Her map can be displayed in a thousand possible ways, most of them only understood by So, but the main one is the master globe of the world. At her touch it slowly revolves, every pixel of it resizable to greater detail, containing everything we've scraped together about King Ruin's infrastructure.

It is a mass of red lines, like one of those balls Art used to make by wrapping elastic bands on top of each other. These are the bond lines of King Ruin's Courts, and they are everywhere still, smothering the world like a cocoon, except for two small patches that are empty.

This spot in the Hollow Desert, and Calico.

It's taken us a year to come this far.

Our greatest advances came in the days after King Ruin's fall, when his Courts and his loyal 'brood' were in shock. We ran a flash raid on Calico via Dactyl helicopters, taking out old Courts and brood-members with mindbombs and dry-ice blasts. There were another ten or so hydrate rigs repurposed as Courts spread around within range of Calico, several buildings even in the center of the city, and a whole suburb that was gradually being turned.

Saunderston.

They'd had it for years, it seemed. I'd ridden trains past it many times along the Wall, but each time they'd Lagged the memory of what I'd seen; Lagged it from everyone that rode by. They'd had their victims skinned and strung up on lamp-posts; hanging out of skyscraper windows knotted limb to limb like links in a chain; bolted to the street while younger brood members raced cars amongst them, scoring points.

When we hit them they were dizzy from the King's partial death, and we razed their home to the ground. We saved what we could, killed all his children and healed the bonds.

It was in Saunderston that I died for the first time, a lucky shot from a panicking Hawk. I got over it. We've shut down hundreds of

Courts like it since then, freeing thousands of victims, but the battle lines scarcely bend. It's a slow, grinding attrition, just like the War, clearing one Court at a time while trying to hold onto the territory we've carved out for ourselves.

"No sign they see us coming," So says in my head. "All three villages are quiet. I'm reading heat signatures underground spreading for hundreds of feet. They have dozens of people down there, and from the flyover it looks like they've got some War-era artillery."

I read the map through So's eyes: three villages of baked adobe clay that have been sitting there for thousands of years. Probably human civilization first sprang up near here. Each of the villages is spaced only a short distance apart, part of an old trading hub circled around an oasis, and each has a well leading down into natural underground caverns, which is where the Court will be.

"Movements in the last few days?" I ask aloud.

"Nothing more than usual," So answers, "some covered wagons went hut to hut selling spiced meat earlier. The people above have no idea what's lurking underneath."

I nod, though only Ray can see it. They'll feel it. We've seen this a dozen times already: a settlement with a Court right underneath, with the brood preying on them person by person. Sometimes it's very slow, farming the villagers like livestock and giving them time to repopulate. These are the brood-members who don't even believe I'm real, like a bogeyman in the night. I know who they are from the sudden terror in their minds when they see me crashing in; they never thought it would happen to them.

Others do believe, and when they realize I'm coming they either flee or they plunge into suicidal, end-of-days decadence. All we find of these latter Courts are the charnel ruins of a bloody orgy that lasted until all the living playthings were dead and the brood-members pulled their own plugs, going off like brilliant fireworks on the bonds. Only rarely do they put up a fight, but their outdated weaponry's no match for us, and it never lasts long.

As for the rest of the King's brood, all the many thousands spread across the world, they're still fighting a cold civil war to fill the power vacuum his half-death left behind. We can glimpse it in the shuffling of bonds, as new generals vie for control of the Suns' global empire.

We're lucky it's taken them so long. If they had united and readied an army at once they could have erased us like they'd erased every insurgency before. Thank Ritry Goligh they did not. It's given us the time to clear their fringe, consolidate our base of power and grow stronger.

I cycle out of So and reach further down, to the open fourth floor bay in the middle of the suprarene, where Yena and her fellow survivor Naji lead the Wall; a group of fifty warriors spread out in EMR bays. I open the eyes of a hand near to her, and she notices at once.

Yena is a survivor of the King's 'glass menagerie', a unique kind of 'zoo' in this very tank where he kept people trapped for years in tiny glass coffins, forced to stare lidlessly into each others' eyes. He was always fascinated by the devastating effects of proximity. She is still broken in many ways, but she is also one of the strongest people I've met, and her knowledge of the King's pyschology is unparalleled.

She's also beautiful, with dark skin and long flowing hair, but beauty is not the thing that draws me to her most. There is something about her pulse on the bonds that inspires me. Before the menagerie she tried to lead a resistance movement against King Ruin, after detecting his presence through warping effects on her EMR research. Nobody believed her, though, and she had nothing to fight with when the King scooped her up.

Now she has me.

"How's the Wall holding?" I ask.

The Wall spreads like a bright bond bubble to encompass our suprarenes, an EMR-shield maintained by our army. This is a trick we learned from the brood; the same way they hid Saunderston from us along with countless other Courts. Multiple minds work in concert to hide us on the bonds, meaning no enemy can know where we are or what we're doing at any time.

The Wall. Yena often runs it. I don't need to ask how it's going, but I like to.

"Holding strong," she says. "Me, try not to die this time."

I smile. "I don't even notice it now." I close the hand's eyes and shift again.

Back at the prow I feel Ray slot back into himself moments after me. He's in charge of the suprarene tanks, four of which we salvaged from the brood, and second wave assault, so he'll have been handing out last-minute orders. He doesn't like it that I take point on these raids, it's not the captain's job, but who cares what he thinks, really? I don't want any of the others to have to die.

Beyond Ray I feel the others: Far tucked into his 50th floor apartment back in the Calico Reach, searching through the aether for some unknowable truth; La churning through the sand beneath us in her subthonic, a deep drill that delves beneath the sand like my old subglacic went beneath the ice; Ti out in the Arctic patrolling the waters we have claimed for ourselves with her two subglacics and an ancient commandeered battleship,

"It's just another mission," Ray says. "Another, and another."

"Hoorah," I reply.

"We're getting closer. We'll find his trail soon."

I grunt something non-committal. The bonds that encircle the world still stink of King Ruin, the half of him that escaped Doe's blast, and he's learned quickly. He keeps his own Walls up everywhere. We've tried to hunt him through the bridge, but more golden shields pop into existence every day. We'd hoped intelligence from his brood-children might help us, but every time we find them they've been Lagged to mindless soup. To date we've cleared one patch of desert and one patch of water, but that means nothing because every day they're uniting more around the remnant of the King. We need to find this new heart and blow it to bits.

"Agreed," says Ray, listening in on my thoughts. "With bells on."

"Come through slow," I tell him. "Wait 'til we've blown the artillery. Then sweep in with holy hellfire."

He grins wide. It's not as impressive as it used to be when he had tooth-piercings, but now there's that tattoo by his eye, which accentuates when he winks.

"I know the routine."

"You should wink more," I tell him as I start back toward the flight deck. "It suits you."

"Yes, sir," he says, and flashes me a big one.

The suprarene engines grind up a pitch underfoot, and the whole structure yaws backward as the great caterpillar treads climb a final dune. I roll with it as smooth as an arene and clatter swiftly down the cage-metal steps to the helicopter deck. My dual-rotor Dactyl, a huge black War-era beast, waits for me on the landing pad, firing up its blades.

In the payload bay stand ten hands dressed in black marine garb, all with King Ruin's buzzing EMR helmets keyed to transpond to my thoughts. I climb in amongst them and pick up my Kaos rifle, affix the bayonet and check my bandolier for ideation grenades.

I might have given a speech to a marine team like this back in my Arctic War days, but these people are all me now, all controlled by my thoughts, and I'm really going in alone.

"Right behind you," says Ray.

"Beneath you," says La.

Hell yes, I think. This is a war, after all.

The helicopter lifts off. I send two hands to man the howitzers, two to man the Bofors miniguns while the rest line up at the rappel drop lines, then I take over the pilot's mind and send us roaring out over the sand, nose down toward the enemy.

2. DACTYL

My Dactyl eats up the distance in taut seconds and I feel the rush begin to build within me, anticipating the carnage to come. Sand tears by, dunes rise up and down like waves. I've died three times by now, though in truth it's more like thirty. I always go with a squad of ten hands and I feel it as each one of them dies. I've died so many times that the line between death and life has become meaningless.

"Steady now," comes Ray's voice in my mind.

"Steady," I repeat, holding the Kaos rifle close.

I surge us low over a dune crest to look down on the spread of three villages. Each is a cluster of tan adobe huts hand-shaped from ancestral mud, centuries old and etched out along some ancient line of best fit, like stars in Orion's belt.

"Frag incoming," So calls, and a second later the sand just to my right cloud-bursts with a ringing-

BOOM

-throwing a backdraft of golden dust skittering off the Dactyl's hull and blowing us off to the side.

I ramp up the throttle, bank sharply left and use the eyes of my hand squatting over the Bofors controls to sight the exact location of the Court's two War-era artillery pieces. They could be fighting in a pre-tsunami world for all their tech level has kept up out here.

Our missiles drop, and while I swerve a sharp zigzag course down the sandy valley toward the first village, the explosions ring out.

BOOM

BOOM

"Qualified," So calls, reading from her aerial heat-graph. "You took them both."

"Diving," I call back, though there's no need as they can all see with my eyes.

The howitzers whirr up and I strafe low over the first village with my fingers on the triggers, sweat beading down my many chests. I'd drop a mindbomb if I thought it was needed, but there's nobody here. Even the artillery pieces were automated.

"Looks like an orgy site," I call back to So. "Seeking confirmation."

She reads the heat-map and sonar, delicate instrumentation mounted to the belly of my Dactyl, while I swoop in low toward the second village, my downdrafts blowing sand into the guttering crater where the first artillery piece had stood. It is molten slag already, incinerated by one thousand-degree-plus temperatures.

"Clear," she says, "Court entrance is ahead of you in the last village."

I tear above the second village in a flurry of chopped rotor beats, like a cavalry stampede with howitzers spinning like fans, but no resistance emerges.

"Deserted," I call, and nose-down toward the third. It's no different from the others, except here we know there's a rough spiral staircase dug into the walls of a natural sinkhole cave, down which all the villagers have been surely transported. "We didn't see the evacuation on recon?"

"Only the meat-cart going around," So says grudgingly, "but maybe they were picking them up."

"They were picking them up," I grunt, and jerk the Dactyl to a landing so hard in the midst of the third village that one of the landing skids cracks.

I don't care; even before it hits my hands are piling out, finding cover and drawing beads on every dark opening into these abandoned huts. We rush in to dark, dingy rooms of mud and straw one after another, and in each of them I see the same thing I have seen at all the orgy-Courts; everything left as it was, frozen at the moment the people were taken.

There are clay-plate meals at dirty plastic crate-tables, dishes in the bucket-sink, bright clothes hung out on long lines from the ceiling to dry away from the bleaching sun. There are neatly folded bedrolls and a few battered hand-me-down toys on the dirt floor and ceramic pots half-filled with winter rice. Usually there is a message for me on a wall in every hut, written in some poor bastard's blood.

RITRY GOLIGH IS NOT A GOD

Many of them do this now, like a welcome mat or a message of defiance. I don't know why, because I never claimed I was.

I hate the orgies the most, not because there are so many dead or because the suffering is so intense, but because this is what his brood do when they've given up. They roll belly-up underground and wait for Ritry Goligh to descend like the hammer of a god they don't believe in, all the while debasing themselves in squalid pleasures, amping up the suffering even as their terror grows.

It's pathetic that this is all they know, and all they want. This is the limit of their ambition.

I've tried to communicate with them so many times, to offer terms in advance, but they won't listen. They clam up, hunker down with a hall full of Souls to scrape away at and wait for me to come, until at the last moment they Lag themselves to soup, too cowardly to be taken my prisoner.

Fuck them all. I hate every last one for the arrogant, sick, pathetic parasites they are. This time I'll charge in to the hilt and extract at least one of them alive, and if not alive, then I'll keep some shred of their thoughts intact, so I can finally fix a location and drop the bomb where I ought, on the resurgent remnant of King Ruin and call this whole attritive war a day.

My ten hands sprint out of their huts while in the distance the slow rumble of Ray's suprarenes draws closer. We hit the rough-cut spiral well staircase at a run with me in the lead, racing down to what must be an adapted tsunami bunker. The steps are large and unevenly cut, the work of generations' past, smacking loudly as my many-booted feet go down them.

I flick up my front-lights as we drop into darkness, all white glare and echoing footfalls. I am a millipede edging in to the core of a rotten apple, and now I begin to feel the villagers trapped in this Court; perhaps fifty in all, all dying and in pain, with perhaps two or three brood-members sitting in judgment. The fact that they are going to die soon helps a little, as the suffering will end. Still I'll have to clean up the ruined bonds of fifty tortured Souls.

At the bottom of the staircase we run along a natural tunnel through chunky basalt, strip-lit in places with flickering yellow halogens. It reminds me of Spartan's Crag out in the Arctic, where so much of this began.

The first body we come to has been partially skinned and submerged in a barrel of salt, enough to keep it screaming. It was a woman but now she's just pink meat and muscle; I shoot her in the head to end the pain. She falls silent, but as I run by an ideation mine buried somewhere in her barrel blows, and several of my platoon are wiped out. The blast sends me crashing into the wall and rocking onto my knees, but it's not enough to take me down.

Ideation mines work where mindbombs cannot, operating not on an electromagnetic level but through hormonic overload; the blast fractures armor while releasing a cloud of weaponized chemical hormones which pour through the fracture gaps. These chemicals work the opposite effect of shock-jacks on the human nervous system, accentuating whatever emotion they've been keyed to. Taken full-bore, they can turn a Soul insane and start them firing upon their own people within seconds, and Electro-Magnetic Resonance helmets do nothing to stop them.

I have the bridge, though, and my link to the others through the aether keeps me focused and running. I am more than one set of senses and one single mind and that's enough to ground me, but still I feel adrift for a few dizzy moments as the dying woman's pain is amplified and blown across my body, rushing in through my nose, eyes, ears, lungs and skin. I feel her terrible pain and it almost overwhelms me. We take suppressant pills against this, we've made the suits and EMRs as airtight as we can, but the brood have been adapting their mines too, and something always gets through.

The connection to several of my hands cuts off as the blast backwashes off the walls; they're lost now and unreliable. A chunk of sand fused to glass emerges from my chest plating, tickling my ribs within, but I've had worse.

Six of us stand, put bullets in the heads of our flailing fellows then storm forward two by two. Rifle fire barks from the dim tunnel's end, a woman and a child who must be hands of the Court, but they fall under our return salvo. We leap over their corpses and corner into a broad, wide, hellish cavern.

All the villagers are here, some fifty bodies laid out in a dark and rough-hewn cave like penitents in some vision of hell; all in barrels of salt, all screaming, no doubt all rigged to blow, and I see this for what is it.

A grand ideation trap.

It'll be the fifth in as many weeks, and it'll be just as much a waste as all of them, unless...

I feel Far, hunkered down in his 50th floor bunker in Calico's rain-soaked Reach, send a galvanic hook out into the universal aether. It isn't anything more than a kind of trace, bondless thoughts he surrenders like I once gave up Arcloberry to the Lag, but it should gravitate toward me. I am just the placeholder in this, now, needed to tag the brood members so Far can track their Souls.

I can feel them ahead of me now, EMR-helmeted against any incursion on the bonds, waiting for me to take the step forward into ideation that will fry this six-tone chord to bits. They're wondering why I haven't.

"Got something," Far calls, and yanks on the galvanic thread, setting his hook. It leads to a tiny gold-shielded constellation in the aether. All this is experimental, a new kind of Soul-grapnel we've never tried before, but it might just work.

Now it falls to me to put these bastards out of their misery.

Silently I send the order and my chord of six hands charges as one. The first rank of barrel-bodies explode with hormonic overload, blasting me with their pain, but pain holds no fear for me after what I've been through, only disorientation, and I charge through it like the Bathyscaphe plunging into a Molten Core. I run on and the next rank blows and the next, and with each ideation blasted over me I slow a little more.

Through the chaos I pick out the brood-members at the head of this awful congregation, a woman and a man standing in strange robes atop a low pallet-stage. They are holding hands, proud and blood-soaked and righteous in what they have done, and I hate them. I hate them so much I love it, can't get enough of it or of what I'm about to do.

At the seventh line of barrels I am perhaps within range, but barely staggering. Who am I, I'm not quite sure. I hate them, but who is it that I hate? These two before me have concern on their faces, they look so wholesome but for the blood that covers their arms and chests.

kill them

-comes the little voice in my head, and I remember what I have to do just long enough to do it, before they can Lag their brains to gray soup in gray skull bowls. I raise my Kaos rifle and send two bullets through each of their heads, pop pop, ten thousand miles an hour and fast enough to outrun the mulching they're hoping for, fast enough that when they die and their gold shields implode so their Souls can release, Far may just be able to hook something of what they are before they dissipate into the aether.

Soul Killer

I drop to the floor as they drop ahead of me and the last of the hall erupts in the hormones of skin-searing pain, engulfed by such a familiar sensation I almost welcome it, and-

got them

-comes the little voice, and-

got you

-it comes, before I die for the fourth time.

3. CALICO REACH

I jerk awake in the gray of Far's bunker, at the top of a Calico Reach tower panting hard, and kick out of the augmented EMR machine as its-

thump thump

-winds down. I'm disoriented and spin to take in my surroundings. The room is simple and plain, just like my old jack-site on the Skulks of proto-Calico. Adapted jacking gear lines the gray walls. There's the acrid stink of Cerebro-Spinal Fluid in the air and the precision feel of Far on the bonds.

"Did you find him?" I croak, not fully certain of what the words mean.

Far's sitting by my side in the space Carrolla once occupied for Ritry Goligh, just coming out of the jack that caught me in the aether. He wears the body of a handsome young man now, dark-haired with a grizzled stubble beard and deep blue eyes that have looked too long into the aether.

"Far, did you find something?"

Far blinks back at me. He has grown into this new face and body in ways I could never have expected. He's clinical and fixated in a way I can barely fathom.

"The mines were stronger," he says, focusing on me. "It's too soon to tell. But maybe."

"Maybe?" I repeat, as I swing my legs, new legs I've never seen before but now *my* legs, off the birthing table and down to touch the ground for the first time. I always do this, hoping to outrun the Disjunct, though I know it will catch up to me in moments. "Do we have a location?"

Those are the words I mean to say, anyway. What comes out is more of a stream of nonsense, as the patterns of my diffused consciousness flow awkwardly through the corridors of a new hollow hand's Molten Core. This is the Disjunct; the burst of power that releases upon death and spreads the Soul to the aether.

Being gathered in from that spread is like rousing from a deep jack in a foreign Core, only to find the gray matter of my brain out of sync with my Soul. Here is the area for producing speech, here is the motor area, here are all the neurons and wiring that make up the hardware of a brain, just as they should be; I recognize them, know them, but my Soul needs to recombine and remember how to run them before I can think smoothly.

King Ruin's hands have all been cored clean to help him control them, but none are a perfect fit for my whole consciousness, especially after it's been fragmented by death. For an instant only I was shooting outward in an amorphous cloud of dissipating thought in the aether, heading to wherever Souls ultimately go…

Then Far gathered me in, like the three times he has before. Now I'm like a newborn, like Ritry Goligh as he woke in his subglacic from the EMR coma that killed his crew. The world is a chaos of jumbled, unordered meaning, and I only grow more baffled as I try to stamp meaning onto it. I sway in position as the incoming signals from my eyes and ears overwhelm my thoughts and the world washes to gray.

"It may be a link to the King," Far says, patting my shoulder in time with the words, aiding in the synchronization, but still it all comes to me in a too-fast jumble. "We don't know."

My pulse surges. "Where is he?" I try to say, though I barely remember who I'm asking about, and the words come out as drool down my chin.

"We'll know soon," says Far, patting my shoulder still, reminiscent of someone else who used to do this for some other incarnation of me so long ago. "We'll have more soon. Take your time."

He helps me up, my legs like jelly, and guides me to the reclined sonic bath chair at the edge of the room, looking out of the window. To me all these sensations now come as a strange lump, but a familiar one. I've run this particular route three times already, from EMR to chair to look at this rain-gray city beyond the glass, and there is some familiarity.

Far settles me into the seat and guides my head into the sonic bath. Slowly he chimes up the simple sound that will help synchronize my drifting mind with my physical body, massaging in the single tone of what I am.

Me.

I let myself succumb, while thoughts of King Ruin and a cavern full of screaming skinless Souls are gently soothed from the burning cells of my Molten Core.

I wake hours later, silent and watching.

The Arctic skies are sediment-gray beyond the glass, turning steadily toward a bitter purple dusk. One of the floor-to-ceiling windows is slightly ajar, and through it I smell Calico, like melting ice and ancient dust, even up here in the Reach. The city lies gray before me, all concrete and steel blotted with portions of green; parks I once took my children to play in. Even death can't steal the weight of Ritry Goligh's memories.

I look across the gap to the neighboring building; a tower just as tall as this, partitioned by floors and apartments, and run my gaze slowly across. Three floors from the top, five from the edge is the window where they still live. This is the perfect sight to wake to after death, to remind me what I'm fighting for.

Ritry Goligh's family.

I see them sometimes through Far's eyes; opening the curtains in the morning, drawing them closed in the evening. They follow a normal day-night cycle like cogs in a machine. Sometimes my daughter Mem stands at the window and looks out into the neon lights and darkness beyond, through what must be her reflection on the bright inner glass. She's seven years old and taller now; in her hand she sometimes holds a doll dressed like a ballet dancer. It breaks my heart to see her like that, waiting for her father to come home.

Waiting for me, or the man I was once a part of. Ritry Goligh. I feel it on the bonds sometimes; thinking if she watches long enough she might just see him coming home. Sometimes Art will stand with her, and Loralena too, a glass of wine in her hand, pressing herself against her children in an act of loving consolation, as if they can ever heal when they don't even know what the wound is.

I don't know if this wound will ever heal. I don't know if the chord can ever go back to being the man they knew. With Doe forever gone and the brood still out there, I can't imagine what the future holds.

Far rests a hand on my shoulder and speaks across the bonds to us all.

"Looks like rain."

Ray snorts in my head. They have jokes between them that are not even jokes. It can be enough sometimes to say words, I suppose.

"Let me know when you get some sun," Ray answers.

Things are different for us now. The world is so much bigger; wider than the War, wider than Mr. Ruin. I see it through six sets of eyes, hear it through six sets of ears, feel it through six layers of skin. Ray has his own life. I have my own life which will continue despite the four times I've died. We all coast on the surface of each other's minds, but we are not one mind anymore, we are not Ritry Goligh.

The Becoming, we call it. We weren't reduced when Ritry Goligh pulled us out of himself; we Became something new.

"What did you find?" I ask.

"Tracks," Far answers, "maybe a correlation."

My heart rate quickens. "And So?"

So answers. I see her on a rare break from her map room, going down to the open deck of the Wall where Yena stands over the corpses of the dead brood members, reclaimed from their Court. They lie in augmented EMR machines, thumping endlessly as we try to capture some trace patterns from their partially-Lagged brains.

"They cored themselves almost completely," she says, "even before you shot them, but along with the scraps Far hooked I think we've got something. You need to be here, Me. We're closing in on a potential location for the King."

My heart thumps like an EMR. "Where?"

"Get here," says So and kills the link.

I push myself up from the sonic bath, forcing this body's unfamiliar, unsteady muscles to work. My mind feels like it's sloshing in a low-brimmed cup and might spill out at any time, but that's a sensation only, not a real concern. I haven't had the top of my head cut off since King Ruin.

A correlation could change everything.

I turn to Far. He's my height now, not the boy he once was. I know he doesn't approve of this, my dying and flitting back and forth between bodies, as with every jack through the aether we give more hints to the brood on how it might be done. I don't approve of what he's doing though either, the way he delves deeper into the aether all day and all night, dancing with the Lag like it's his best friend.

These thoughts pass between us smoothly and naturally. These are our addictions and our choices.

"Send me back," I say.

He turns and gestures to the EMR. With his help I lurch to the machine and slide inside. I close my eyes and wait for Far to pull me out through the bridge, toss me across the world to the orange deserts of Darain and slot me into the waiting body of a new hand in the belly of Ray's suprarene.

It will make the headache worse. I'll have another new body to adjust to, but it's nothing compared to the Disjunct, because I haven't died this time and a little discomfort won't bother me. More than anything, I feel surging hope. For a year now we've been hunting the remnains of King Ruin across the bonds and the bridge, through Courts, mindbombs and ideation mines and this is the first hint of his location we have found. Perhaps it will lead us to his beating Solid Core deep in the ruins of his broken empire, and show us the brood member that's helping him resurge so we can blow them both to fucking dust.

Far shucks me out of this body, I see the glinting dust and crackling purple stars of the aether for a few brief seconds then I'm zooming in to a landing.

4. SUPRARENE

I open my eyes in the suprarene's belly.

It's dark but for low yellow downlights illuminating the floor. Reorienting myself briefly, I look up at the riveted ceiling, etched with the faint shadows of bolts. This is the deck where King Ruin once kept his glass menagerie. Now we keep the spare hands here, lying in subterranean dark to wait for the moment we call them to service.

I click back the glass lid of my pod and a hiss of gas escapes. There's no one to welcome me in, but then this is the fourth time I've done this and I don't need a welcome party. I send a silent thanks back to Far but he's already gone, jacked ahead to a temporary hand on the Wall deck above.

I climb out of the pod feeling like a marine freshly forged in the Bathyscaphe, my new copper skin near-black in the low lights. Padding to a plastic trunk nearby I find the standard gray jumpsuit of all hands waiting for me. The clothes smell fresh as the day they were woven, probably three decades past. I pull them on, snap the captain's star into place then take a long swig of water, which should help with the migraine.

Too many jumps, Far would say. Every jump you expose yourself. It worries me, but the brood still haven't managed to jack the bridge, though they've been trying for a year. Some came close but they all flamed out at the Solid Core blast door, unable to handle the enormity of the aether. Each time we felt them burst like rotten fruit, their deaths washing over us all.

They're learning, Far warns. But then so are we.

I head to the deck elevator and step by step my Soul locks into command of this new nervous system, pushing the migraine aside. I take a last look back at the hand-pods stretching into darkness behind me, taking up a whole deck of the suprarene; they're half empty already. Soon we'll run out of pre-cored hands, and I don't like to think about what we'll do then. We have to finish the King and the brood before we reach that point...

The elevator arrives and I crank the grille open, step in and set it grinding up toward the Wall, feeling the buzz of excitement in the bonds fuming down from Yena and Ray and So, along with the thump thump of the Wall. Decks pass me by with stenciled signs:

HABITATION

HYDROPONICS

ARMORY

HOSPICE

In a minute I'm there, looking out over the dim blue glow of the Wall. It encompasses a whole deck; a networked array of one hundred bulky Electro-Magnetic Resonance machines, all locked into a unified cycle that thumps like the pulse of a giant and charges the air with a molten flow of electrostatic.

THUMP THUMP

THUMP THUMP

THUMP THUMP

A hundred of the King's survivors man it, each lying in the donut hole of their own EMR with an operative watching on, each trained in basic Soul jacking techniques. It affords us our main defense against attack on the bonds, blotting us from prying eyes.

Faint blue light spills from each EMR monitor station, outlining the block-grid of alleys between these hulking plastic-metallic machines like the pathways through a Skulk. Through floor-to-ceiling windows at the edges the desert burns like a russet torc as the sun goes down.

There's no more time to waste.

I stride between the EMRs, each as big as a forging pod, to find Ray, So and Yena standing in person around a holograph desk, with Far, La and Ti present through hands. They're all looking at an interweaving cloud of lights hovering above the desk; some kind of map. Yena looks up and I feel her excitement on the bonds.

"We've got him," she says, her dark eyes wide and lustrous. "This could be it."

"Tell me," I say.

So taps the desk and the complex holograph simplifies to a three-dimensional representation of the aether, with thousands of purple points of light representing Souls, many now shrouded with shimmering gold shields.

"I never learned to read this," Ray mutters suspiciously.

"This is Far's map of the aether," So says, even as she expertly works controls to set the map spinning. "As we all know, the King used to be at the center." The middle of the map highlights, and the ghosts of two spiraling suns appear within. A swift animation plays out, as the tiny figure of Doe approaches one of the Suns and explodes, triggering a blast wave that leaves only one Sun remaining, which fades then simply winks out.

So looks up. "We've been looking for where that half of the King went ever since Doe killed his twin, but we were acting on bad information. Pieces of the aether, pieces of the real world, but never enough to correlate the two. Now though we have a physical trace from the last Court, *and* we have Far's hook on the aether."

I raise one eyebrow. "You've got the correlation?"

"Yes," says So, and brings up a map of the Hollow Desert to overlay the aether; dunes, rock and villages over stars and bond-lines. She works a few controls that warp the two maps, bringing them into some kind of union. I watch in awe as the maps ripple and flex organically, latching on like an octopus' suckers. "It's more art than science," So goes on, "but you're looking at it." She looks up at me and grins proudly. "I'm confident we can infer geographical location from topographical locus in the aether."

I look at Ray. He's grinning widely too. I'm not sure either of us understand this wholly.

"Give it to me plain."

"We found the King on the aether," So says. "He's right here."

A spot on the map flares red. It doesn't mean anything to me, but it could be everything. I stare at the purple hues continually blurring and bending over sand as the map realigns in line with some unseen algorithm.

My mouth is dry. "Where is that?"

"Lefkandi," says So, a word I don't recognize. "It's an ancient town on the Ohkotsk Sea at the edge of the Hollow Desert, just seventy kilometers from here. Once it was a graveyard of empires, thousands of years ago. All that remains are some ruined statues to ancient heroes, buried in the sand. Here." She sweeps away the twisting flow of the aether, leaving only the desert and the spot at the edge glowing red.

I try to frame words. We've searched for so long.

"It's a locus of extraordinary strength in the aether," So says, "massively shielded and incredibly dense, one of just a few such sites anywhere. We're confident this is him. But it's not only him." A second red dot flashes up alongside the King; exceeding his brightness. "This doesn't correspond to any brood member we know, but it's a very powerful Soul. Its probably the reason we haven't been able to track the King; this location doesn't correspond to any escape vector the King might have taken on his own, but..."

My excitement surges as the missing piece falls into focus. I can see it in the twin flashing blips, like new orbiting Suns. We've been reading their growth on the bonds all this time and watching them surge; this Soul was just the first and the best.

"You're telling me the King didn't escape on his own. One of the brood dragged him here."

"Exactly," So says. A moment passes as this sinks in. "The strongest brood-member we've yet seen."

I gaze at the map's flashing dots and feel something close to divine grace fall upon me. Maybe this is it.

"Ritry Goligh," I murmur.

"That's what I said," says Ray.

I look up at Far. "Do they know we know?"

He shakes his head. "I doubt it. They haven't passed through the bridge yet, so they've no way of knowing what we've seen and what we haven't."

I lick my dry lips, thinking all the ramifications through. This is what we've been waiting for. This is the closest we've come to their heart, enough to blow the old network of bonds to shreds and break them all in one fell swoop. I gauge the distance on the map, then look up and see all eyes on me. Seventy clicks by Dactyl would make us too visible, would take an hour at least and they'd have time to relocate. The suprarenes would take all day.

I turn to La's hand, thinking of her subthonic burrowing deep underground. "Can you do it in a day, La? Can you surface silently?"

"I can do it in a night," she says. "Come up hard with the dawn. We'll be on them while they're taking their morning piss."

This is it, then. One more night and the war could be over. "Do it. I'll lead the attack." I turn, building out the whole of the assault. "Ray, merge the suprarenes into a standard defensive diamond right here, giving nothing away. Ti, you'll be on high alert for reprisals. Far, prepare to throw more hooks out; I'm done hunting and I don't want any of these bastards to escape again."

I look round at them. They look back at me.

"It's just another Solid Core," I say. "We've done this a thousand times before. Any questions?"

There are no questions.

"Get ready. Get some rest, if you can. Tomorrow we end this war."

I stride out of the hall.

Two decks up I stand on the suprarene's open top. The night air smells like desert orchids and distant thunder. I walk along the metal grille amongst my Dactyls, their cooling engines clicking soothingly in the night air, to the forward prow platform. There I look out over the dune horizon, faint and dark but crested with silvery lines of moonlight glinting off sand, like froth on the Arctic waves.

In a day we may have King Ruin. It's hard to imagine. We've come so far since the days of the Skulks. Words from the last Court come back to me.

RITRY GOLIGH IS NOT MY GOD

They write it at the scenes of their orgies when all they really want is a god to lead them forward. I've tried to reason with them but they won't listen. I've killed them and they've killed me and the battle line barely changes. King Ruin's empire cannot be reasoned with or tolerated in some diminished form; it can only be destroyed.

I'm going to have to wipe them out.

The dunes are beautiful like this, but they do nothing to change the darkest secrets they hide, a thousand Courts buried underneath. How many innocents will die before it's done?

Yena comes to stand by my side. She can't read my thoughts, she knows nothing more than what I show from the outside, but here she is.

"So many stars," she says, leaning her head against my shoulder. This simple action stirs a welter of emotions and I turn to her. She is beautiful for her strength, an example to us all. In many ways she is stronger than me. She survived in the glass menagerie for years, driven by hope in the face of all-consuming despair.

I stop thinking and kiss her. She folds into my arms like she has always belonged there. We are both so damaged that it feels like communion. This is what being a tone of Ritry Goligh should feel like; this is the love we all seek. In these moments I don't think of

Loralena or my children waiting halfway across the world, I only think about Me.

They will wait for Ritry Goligh. One day when we win this war I'll try to go back, to Become some version of Ritry Goligh again and go home, but for now I need this. In my quarters a deck below we kiss and sink onto the bed, and into each other, and begin to move in slow, sweet, aching tandem.

5. ERUPTION

I wake long before dawn, stirred by the movements of the chord. Far is deep through the bridge and scanning the aether, So is intent upon her maps, Ray is running checks on all the suprarene cannon and La is drawing close to Lefkandi in her subthonic.

I nudge Yena's leg from my own and rise. It wouldn't be fair for her to wake and find this body unconscious beside her, absent my presence. I kiss her on her cheek, she murmurs, then I'm out and padding down the dark metal corridor toward the Wall.

"Report," I say through the bridge as I ride the slow industrial elevator up from the barracks.

"T-minus ten kilometers," La replies. "We're rising at fifty feet per hour, so far avoiding bedrock. I think we're on course to surface in thirty minutes, an hour before the dawn."

"Good," I reply, "are you ready for me?"

"Your chord's laid out."

"Far?"

"Ready," he says.

It's enough. My heart starts to thump, pumping adrenaline into this body. Today I'm going to see King Ruin again. He tore me to pieces. He's the reason Doe had to die. Now I'm going to keep all the promises I made while he tortured me in his white room, and tear him to shreds.

The elevator opens on the Wall, still at this hour but for the immense thump thump of so many EMRs. Ray is waiting for me, big and dark though he's not so big and not so dark anymore. He pulls me into an embrace with no need to talk.

"Yena?" he asks.

"Sleeping," I say. "Are we in position?"

"Tanks are in a standard defensive diamond well within our territory, nothing that should raise suspicion. Unless they've got radar that can see underground they'll have no idea we're coming."

I nod. He nods.

I get into the nearest EMR and pass through the bridge, opening my eyes near-instantly in another hand, in the subthonic one thousand feet underground with La looking down at me.

"Captain," she says.

"La," I answer, rolling out of the bay. There's no headache because I haven't fully crossed over, keeping my Soul back on the suprarene. This is more like remote controlling a hand than occupying it. It means a little delay in my motor control, but that's the price I pay for the element of surprise.

I look down and see they've decked me out in segmented black armadillo armor already; I may as well have forged to life inside the Bathyscaphe.

I look around the subthonic's hand-bay, a place I've only faintly sensed through La before. It's dark, dank and squat, rimmed and shaped by pipes, even tighter than our sublavic. The grind of the forward drill reverberates dully through everything, traveling at nearly twenty knots through clean sand. I can feel how happy La is to be here, this place that so closely resembles our old ship. She even looks different, having taken a new body since Becoming. She didn't want to look like her sister anymore, just another reaction to the King. Now she's short, handsome, and I believe she's more promiscuous than Ray, though I try not to pry.

"Your chord," she says, and points to the ten bodies lying in bays either side of me. I reach out and into them, feeling them move beneath my commands. For a moment there is the standard dizzying impetus of so many eyes, ears, and skins flooding into my mind, but in seconds I acclimate. I've done this so many times with so many hands that they just feel like another combat suit.

"Good," I say. "Take me to the con."

"Yes, sir."

My chord and I troop in tandem, following La. I run them through minor calisthenics as we pass up the subthonic's long thin body, stretching their bodies and minds. I have them draw rifles, mime tossing mindbomb grenades and practice sheltering from ideation mines as the grind of the forward drill grows louder.

"We're above the alimentary canal," La shouts over the dull roar. In her mind I see schematics of the subthonic laid out; a Lag-like machine with a heavy jaw-drill at the front, a long hollow tube bored through the middle and out the back, through which chewed-up debris is propelled outward. "We eat sand and shit gold."

I laugh. Another change in La since the Sunken World is she's cruder.

"As long as it gets us there."

We climb a low inclined metal ramp, breathing in the smells of diesel oil and burnt tar, then emerge into the deployment hangar. It's long and low leading up to the conning jaws at the front, with weaponry hanging from webbing in the walls and filled with dark assault vehicles parked in a neat square.

"We've got three groundhogs," La shouts over the drill's roar, patting the haft of each semi-armored vehicle as we pass it; camouflaged orange and brown troop carriers with howitzer mounts on top. I already envision splitting my chord three to two groundhogs each and four to ride with me in the lead.

"And one Jeriko tank," La goes on, striking hard the flat shank of a great hulk of beige metal, spiky with guns, howitzer mounts and a central Bofors cannon. The hollow machine makes a deep bonging sound. "I'll drive it to lay down covering fire."

I look around the bay and feel the adrenaline start to pump afresh. King Ruin is not expecting this. King Ruin and whoever is helping him are going to die today.

La grins, then points up to two great pistons at the far end of the hangar, culminating in huge ball bearings.

"The jaws," she shouts. "Assault plan dictates the the subthonic surfaces at forty-five degrees, the bottom jaw drops to ground level and the top lifts wide to give us clearance. We'll have a straight shot out onto sand."

"Like a shark," I say.

"A full-metal shark," La adds, "spitting out baby sharks. We'll be on them before they even know we've broached their perimeter."

"How many arenes have you got?" I ask.

"Twenty battle-ready that can ride along with you. Ti and I will control them."

It's more than any raid we've gone with since we took Calico. I'd like Dactyls for the sheer maneuverability, but that would show our hand too much. It'll have to be enough.

"So?" I call through the bridge.

"No movement on radar, Me," So answers. "If they know we're coming, they haven't shown it through any major movement."

"Far?"

"The King's still there, and the brood-member with him," he answers. "The aether hasn't shifted."

This is it. I climb my chord into the groundhogs as the subthonic grinds us closer to the surface and the rattling gets louder.

"T-minus one minute," La shouts over the roar. "Brace for eruption."

--.

A. ALONE

The Bathyscaphe is silent.

I wake in my forging pod slumped against the wall, with a stinging pain in my throat and no memory of where it came from. Breathing comes to me raggedly, and I have to labor to get the oxygen in.

I look around, becoming aware of the stillness. The forging pod's flame is long gone and I feel only half-birthed. I'm not all here. I look down and see my black sublavic combat suit stretching down to arms, legs, feet, hands, but something is wrong. There is yellow writing across my chest, written upside down as if it intended for me alone to read.

INFILTRATE THE HOLLOW STAR

The words mean nothing to me. I rub a hand over my chest and the movement dislodges something sickly in my gut. Acid gorges up my throat and I vomit into the drain. Abruptly I'm sweating hard.

"Ray," I say, "Far."

No voices come.

I'm sick. I need help. I lift a numb foot and step into the corridor. My left leg spasms and goes weak, nearly dropping me to the floor, but I catch myself on a damp-stained pipe.

What's happening?

The screw is silent; there's not even the churn of lava or the drip of tsunami water. I look to left and right and see the barren corridor stretching away. The other six forging pods are empty.

"Shit," I whisper.

Another rush comes up my throat and I vomit, then trigger the shock-jacks in my suit. They stir silently to life and quickly I feel some sense of normalcy return as endorphins and adrenaline flood my system. The flash-sweat fades, the trembling ebbs and strength returns to my palsied muscles.

I stride down the corridor looking into each forging pod where my chord members should be. "Ray!" I shout, hoping perhaps they have woken before me. "Doe!"

As her name comes out I remember that she's dead. Of course she is. She died in the aether over a year ago, bringing down half of King Ruin with a supernova suicide, and there was no coming back from that.

The thought makes me sad. I stop at the end of the pods looking at the space where Far should be. Are they all dead? Where are they, and where am I?

My fingers trail across the words on my chest, remembering many messages like this left by Far to guide me on my way. I remember the distant days of Ritry Goligh's War when every jack into a Soul was new. I was only half alive then, really only one seventh alive, and now I am just...

What?

Enough. I break my vapid stare and start for the conning tower; I need answers. I don't have my HUD so I take the measure of the Bathyscaphe through the metal and air as I go: no vibrations from the screw, no familiar stink of burning brick, no watery mud dripping in from a Sunken World. Rather there is only a faint, underlying tang in the air.

Ozone.

I hit the pipes as I go as a signal to anyone else in the ship, tapping out my name in Morse code.

-- .

ME

I aim for the top of the sub but somehow find myself in crew quarters, standing outside Doe's room. I don't know how I got here; it's not on the way to the conning tower. Still I push the door open and peer in, as if I might find Doe inside. For a moment my heart leaps, hoping against hope that she will be here, but...

She's not. Of course she's not. A fresh wave of sickness rushes through me and I take more shock-jacks before my legs give out. There's no Doe here, just a neat regulation bed like an EMR tray deployed from the wall. A wall-locker hangs open and I peer in: a white dress uniform, rank first lieutenant, some ancient sticks of unbranded chewing gum, a plastic flashlight and a penknife. So few things, we leave behind.

I hadn't even realized we had crew quarters on the Bathyscaphe. I'm the captain but I didn't know that, and there's something desperately sad about it. The forging pods are the only place I ever woke. This place is like the echo of a cry that never sounded, more an intention than anything real.

I don't mean to start crying, I only find the tears leaking down my cheeks. To wipe them away would seem crass, too purposeful, so I let them flow. If I was Ritry Goligh now is the time I would find a bottle of vodka and start to drink.

But I'm not Ritry Goligh. I stride in and pick a stick of gum from Doe's locker. I never saw her chewing it. The silver wrapper unfolds like the metal jacket circling a gunpowder round, and the gum slips through my fingers as a desiccated powder. How much time has passed with her gone? All this is like the dreams of a child stumbled upon in later life.

Something is very wrong. I shouldn't be here alone like this. Where the hell are my chord?

I stride out, leaving the gum wrapper behind.

The conning tower lies waiting for me, empty and sterile under raw white lights like a vision of the past. To the right lies So's radar and sonar deck, at the front are Doe's controls for glassbomb and Quantum Confusion foils, to the left are La and Ti's stations for trim tank override, screw readouts, and a dozen minor corrective mechanisms for the fins. Ray would stand at my side with Far in back, and in the middle is the periscope where I belong.

I don't belong there now. I don't know where I should go. I head to the engine screw readout and tap the screens to life. Digital readouts flash red then fade. I follow the ignition process, stamped into my mind like letters into metal, but nothing responds. The Bathyscaphe is dead and without La and Ti there is no way I can repair it.

I press my face to the periscope's rubber eyepiece, expecting to see the churning orange magma of a Molten Core or the writhing black mud of a Sunken World beyond, but it is neither. Rather I see a gray wall of rock, stippled and blotchy like a moon's cratered face. A faint reddish light illuminates it from the side, outlining every pockmark with a shadowy crescent. I swing the periscope to the left, but it clanks hard against something, reverberating back through the metal and into my forehead.

I mutter a curse and try to swing the other way, but get the same clank; the periscope is jammed on rock. I cycle the screen through infras, ultras, radiation and spectrographic seeking a pattern in the rock or the light, but there is no clue in either of them.

I'll have to exit and see for myself.

I head for the captain's hutch. Past the racks of heavy concrete Extra-Vehicular Activity suits and outlandish QC weapons, I duck in and look over the little lockers built into the walls and ceiling. Last time the mission folder was in locker 47, or so I recall, for the proto-Calico Skulk Ritry Goligh lived on.

It won't be that now. I go to the number seven, for seven tones in a chord, but it too is locked. I turn to another locker, perhaps one that more truly represents what I am now.

1.

It opens easily and I pull out the long metal box from within. The lid opens with a twang; inside is a piece of scratchy yellow vellum sketched with some kind of architectural plan; a large arch standing atop two long columns.

It means nothing to me.

I turn the paper and see there are labels on the reverse, written to seemingly match up with the two pillars of the arch.

ME

YOU

I don't know what it means. Maybe nothing. Still I fold the paper and tuck it into an inner suit pocket, then head back to the conning tower. I suit up with Durance packs, candlebomb, a Quantum Confusion pistol at each hip and Doe's bondless accelerator mounted to the shoulder of my suit. Last of all I slip on my HUD, old friend, and whisper into blood-mic.

"Anybody there?"

No answer comes.

I climb the ladder, spin open the inner hatch and outer hatch, and the ship gives a gasp as the seal is broken and the metallic smell of ozone floods in stronger than ever. The inner layer of red brick cladding hangs above me and I hammer into it with the pickaxe. Bricks chip and shatter. I bash my way through one layer, two, three until another hiss sounds as my air escapes outward.

Overhead there is a rock ceiling, as lifeless as the Arctic but for that strange red light. I ask the HUD for an atmosphere report on the atmosphere and it comes back moderate: low levels of oxygen, low nitrogen, low carbon dioxide. There is just enough here to breathe but not one iota more.

I emerge to stand atop the brick back of my sublavic ship, taking in the strange sweep of this place.

It's a huge cave. Strange stalagmites rise up and cradle the Bathyscaphe; strange stalactites hang down and jam the periscope. The walls are rounded rock. I can't see any way in or out; certainly nothing big enough to admit the Bathyscaphe. How did I get here? I feel lonely and weary and sick. The Bathyscaphe's broad back lies like a brick coffin before me, mirrored by something that doesn't even register at first, it's so strange.

Another sublavic ship.

It lies next to mine like a lover, two whales beached within a cave and wrapped up in brick. Thrown by a tsunami, perhaps. Rotting and lost. I don't understand. It doesn't make any sense. As I stare its periscope circles steadily, scanning the rock walls, scanning the Bathyscaphe until finally it settles on me.

B. SOLFEJE

My hand twitches over the QC pistols. I could destroy this ship with a few blasts from Doe's cannon. Whoever's watching me now would die and I'd be safe.

But I don't want to be safe. More than anything I want to find the chord, and maybe the person on that ship can help. I toss the QCs to the brick cladding and unlatch the cannon from its mount on my shouder. It crunches behind me as I advance, palms out.

The periscope tracks my approach.

At the edge of the Bathyscaphe, where the brick cladding corners down too steeply to follow, I stop and wait. The periscope remains steady. Moments pass, then there is the muffled thump of a pick smashing into brick. I wait until a glint of metal breaks through this twin ship's outer cladding, and I wait as the hole widens and a figure climbs out. There's just one, wearing a sublavic suit with QC pistols in hand.

I try a smile then realize this person cannot see my face through the visor. Trust has to begin somewhere. I raise my hands slowly to my HUD and unclasp it. It lifts clear. The air inside the cave is bitter with ozone but breathable.

"What are you doing?" the figure asks, surprised. It's a woman's voice. She doesn't take off her HUD. With my helmet off her QC pistols would dissociate me in seconds, and maybe she finds that alarming.

I smile again. It's not a comfortable moment, but what does that matter? I had all the advantages; my suit, my weapons, the element of surprise, and I gave it all up just to hear her voice. I'm glad not to be alone.

"Making friends," I say. "My name's Me."

"I don't want a friend."

"I can help you. We can help each other."

"I don't need help."

Maybe that's true, maybe not. I don't really know what to say. "Take off your helmet," I try. It's not an order. Not a suggestion, really. Just a next step, because what else are we going to do? I don't think she understands any of this either.

She does it. Slowly, watchfully, waiting perhaps for me to spring a trap or pull a hidden QC, her hands go to her HUD and twist it clear. When I see her face my heart skips a beat. She could almost be Doe returned from death. She has albino-pale skin and near white hair. I remember to breathe. I peer at her closely; of course it isn't Doe. There are differences in her eyes, her cheeks. It's not Doe, because Doe is dead.

"Where's your pulse?" she asks.

It's a good question. I consider lying. I consider the truth, that I wasn't part of a pulse but a seven-tone chord. I settle on a mixture of the two, by omission. "Not here. I don't know where. What about yours?"

Her eyes, a translucent blue so pale it's like looking into ancient glacier ice, bore into me. "Dead. And what do you mean, not here?"

"Didn't come through with me in the forge," I say, careful not to say 'they'. It seems important to keep my seven-tone chord to myself. "I woke up alone. What happened to your other?"

"Died after forging," she says.

We study each other in uneasy détente. The strange reddish light ripples over the rock roof and walls in familiar patterns, like waves from an EMR. I take the moment to rub my eyes.

"What's the 'Hollow Star'?" she asks. It doesn't make sense for a moment, then I realize she's looking at the yellow paint written on my chest.

"I have no idea. It was there when I forged."

She grunts.

"What's your name?" I ask.

"Solfeje. And you?"

"Me."

More gazing, more assessing. "I woke sick," I say, to break the silence. "Not like a usual forging. Alone. I vomited and felt like I was going to die. How did your other die?"

"He vomited to death," she says. Her voice is flat but I sense the emotion underneath. I can make out the reddened marks around her eyes and down her cheeks. Even the most hardened marine can't help but weep like a baby when a part of them gets cut away.

Doe, I think. I know how I felt when we lost her.

"I don't want to die like that," I say. "I don't think you want to either. We could help each other, if our missions align. But first, I'd like to see your other."

She stares at me. "See my other."

"To understand. I'm sick. I want to know what's coming."

She stares at me for a long hard moment, weighing me up. "No QCs. No cannon."

"Same goes for you," I answer.

She stares a moment longer then drops her pistols to the brick cladding. She might have more secreted in her suit, but what does it matter? Whether I'm unarmed in her ship or unarmed in this cave, it doesn't make a difference.

"Come on then."

I make the leap to the back of her ship, landing smoothly. She looks about my height, about my build. If it came down to a brawl I can't say who would win.

"After you," I say, pointing to the gouge she smashed through brick to the ladder leading down. She jumps without taking her gaze off me, straightening perfectly so she slips like a needle through the narrow gap. I hear the thunk as she lands in the conning tower below.

I hadn't expected that. She'll have time to do whatever she wants; prime a trap, ready a shield, but there has to be trust. I could fetch a QC of my own but that would ruin it already.

I climb down the old-fashioned way, hand-over-hand. Her conning tower looks much like mine, though maybe a newer model. The screens look sleeker, the angles better designed, the corners more rounded.

"Nice," I say, standing beside her periscope. "Did you fight in the War?"

Her ice-blue eyes lock on mine like missile sights. "Which war?"

I smile. I'm not sure I remember anymore. "It's always a war, isn't it?"

Her head tilts slightly, then she points. "This way."

She doesn't wait for me. I follow her down a ladder then along narrow corridors constricted by paneled pipes and ducts in the walls, around structural bulkheads, walking in this bubble of tenuous trust.

In silence we pass down a corridor that looks like crew quarters, with names engraved on metal plaques just like on the Bathyscaphe.

Solfeje and Solmiz.

"Do you remember him?" I ask. "Solmiz?"

She answers without turning her head. If having me walk behind her makes her uncomfortable, she doesn't show it. "No. Do you remember yours?"

I think again of Doe; I know there's a tragedy there, but the others have reduced to vague notions now. This place is dimming my mind. I know their names but that is all.

"Not like I should."

She continues on down ladders and along corridors until we come to the forging pods. Even the pipes here look much the same as aboard the Bathyscaphe, painted the same gray color and stained with the same stains.

"Here's mine," she says, pointing to an empty pod, "and here's Solmiz."

He lies curled on the floor of his pod, dressed in the same sublavic suit as Solfeje and just as pale-skinned, though his skin has a sick, waxy sheen. He doesn't look familiar, he just looks dead.

"May I?" I ask.

She gestures to go ahead.

I step into the pod with no clear idea what I'm looking for. I kneel by his side and turn his face slightly. I can see he's been sick.

"How long did it take?" I ask.

"Less than ten minutes. I forged with him already choking. I tried to stop it but I couldn't."

I do a quick calculation in my head, counting how long it took me to leave the Bathyscaphe. "We might have come through at the same time," I say. "To this place, however we got here. Does that mean anything to you?"

"Should it?"

"I don't know." I think hard. "Am I familiar to you? Do you know me? I can't imagine we're here at the same time, in near-identical ships and both alone, by accident."

She looks at me for a long hard moment. "Perhaps. You do feel familiar, but I don't know why."

"You're familiar to me too," I say. "You look like my other."

She frowns. I catch a faint twitch in her throat that tells me she's subvocalizing a suit command on blood-mic, though without a HUD that would be meaningless, unless...

"You're sick too," I say.

"What?"

"I just saw you taking shock-jacks. You've got the same thing. You're sick."

"I'm fine."

"Why lie? We want to fix this. It killed Solmiz. It may kill you and me next. You're sick."

She stares at me, giving nothing away. "Yes, I'm sick. Not like him, maybe not like you, but I'm sick."

I nod, thinking. "It's this place. Or maybe it's the way we came through. Do you think we're in a Solid Core?"

"I don't know. I didn't see anything except the rock."

Here I know she's lying. I don't know how. Something in those eyes, maybe. A different shade of pale.

"We have to tell each other the truth," I say. "Otherwise why not just go duel it out with QCs?"

She stares, gives the slightest of nods, then taps the wall. A rectangle of glass lights up, taking me by surprise. A screen of some kind. Controls flash up and her fingers dance over them, and in seconds a video autoplays. I recognize it at once; a view of my Bathyscaphe from the fore and side, lit by the same red glow rippling off the roof.

I lean in to see better. "This is from your periscope?"

She grunts. "Watch."

I watch. The periscope turns. Hers is not blocked by stalactites so it strafes down a full three-sixty view of the Bathyscaphe, across a barren expanse of rock wall then the screen starts getting brighter. The contrast dials down and the rock turns near-black as the periscope approaches an oblong block of roiling red and orange.

"Look familiar?" Solfeje asks.

I am entranced. It's like looking through the open mouth of an oven into, well…

"It's a Molten Core," I whisper.

"It's not mine," Solfeje says.

I blink. Striations of red and orange billow through the oblong of churning magma like flexing muscle. It isn't possible. Anything that hot would burn through this rock in seconds. The sublavics should be engulfed and the air baked out of existence. We shouldn't be walking around, but somehow we are.

This is no normal mission.

"Then whose Molten Core is it?"

Solfeje taps the screen. Readings pop up; heat, patterns, flows, dimensions. The size of this opening into a living mind is small, definitely not big enough for either ship to fit through, maybe just wide enough for a single person wearing an EVA suit.

I look at Solfeje. "What do you know?" I ask.

"What do you know?" she answers.

I rack my mind. Hollow Star, my chest says. Is that a message from Far? The mission pack from my hutch was just an archway, but that means nothing to me. Still, I can feel there's something important here now. Something that matters very much indeed.

"We need to get out there," I say. "Figure out what that thing is. Where we are. If we're alone."

Solfeje kills the periscope footage mid-revolve, just as I appear in the feed atop the Bathyscaphe. In the second before the image flickers away, I notice her ship's glassbomb forks are tuned and pointing right at the little figure of me.

She was ready to kill us both. It's a good thing I dropped my weapons.

"Let's go," she says.

C. HOLLOW STAR

It takes moments only to climb back up to her conning tower, and from there to the brick spine of the ship. I leap over to the Bathyscaphe and with deliberate slowness pick up my HUD.

I watch Solfeje do the same. We'll need the visors just to go near that window into the Molten Core. She nods, and we both smoothly pull the helmets on. Now the QCs are largely useless again, so it doesn't mean much when I pick mine up and holster them. Hopefully that won't be a problem. Solfeje does the same.

I gesture to the far end of her ship where the hot glow is coming from. "Ladies first," I say, our suits communing via blood-mic.

"Captain's prerogative," she answers. "It's nearer my ship."

Can't argue with that. I leap back to her ship then start back down the spine. The crunch of her footsteps on brick tells me she's following. My back itches to have her behind me, and I pretend not to feel it. There has to be trust.

The light gets brighter as I near the tail fins, and the suit's visor dials darker, protecting my eyes from the glare. Above the screw I halt and Solfeje halts alongside me, both of us looking into the letterbox opening below.

Lava churns within, held back by some unseen barrier.

"There's no way our ships could have come through that," she says.

I grunt agreement. We must have come in some other way. I take the opportunity to give myself another dose of shock-jacks to counteract the growing weakness in my legs. I try not to think of Solmiz, dead in his vomit, and instead point to the pitted rock ceiling.

"You think there's Molten Core on the other side of that too?"
"It would make sense."

I contemplate the outline of such a structure. La or Ti would be better at this. Are we inside a rock inside a Molten Core? Are we in an empty Solid Core?

"I can depth-sound it," I say. It's La and Ti's specialism, but I know the basics. "Gamma radiation should tell us."

Solfeje waves a hand. I pull my grapnel pistol, mount a gamma head and tether it with elasteel, then fire. It thunks into the ceiling and begins transmitting data back to my HUD at once. I sling the feed to Solfeje and we read the streams together.

"It's not a Core of any kind," she says.

"It's nothing."

We both read the feeds. There's a pulse out there, rapid-fire, but other than that it is empty. No echoes come back. There's no heat, no Core, no lava; nothing but empty space.

"The wall's thin," Solfeje says. "It's a rock shell only. Maybe we can blow through and take a better look."

"Maybe," I answer, and for a moment I remember doing something like this before. There was an explosion, a falling horse into lava, then the memory is gone. I point my QCs at the ceiling, Solfeje does the same and we fire in tandem.

Anti-matter particles sloosh out, eat into rock, and through in seconds. At once glaring light sears in through the smooth-bored hole, purple and flashing. I cycle my HUD down against it and peer into the images as they resolve.

I see emptiness, and energy, and drifting matter.

What the…

I grapnel up to the lip of the borehole. Solfeje grapnels in next to me and we both climb carefully through into…

Space.

Stars, blackness and emptiness.

We stand upon a slowly spinning chunk of cratered gray rock, one of thousands of asteroids in a vast conglomerated ring that stretches ahead and behind in some kind of orbital ring, curving hundreds of thousands of clicks around a flickering purple star at the center.

The scale is immense. My jaw drops.

I look in to the purple star, so massive and bright that I can't resolve any details. Every second it pulses three or four times, like a lighthouse transmitting Morse code. I can taste something on those wavelengths, some embedded message like the bonds of memory, but I can't decipher what the meaning is.

In every other direction hangs the empty black void of space, studded with countless distant stars.

"Ritry Goligh," I whisper.

"Indeed," says Solfeje, "and look."

She points. It takes a few seconds to resolve them; out there in the darkness, faintly white when they catch the star's purple pulse, so miniscule they're like hairline cracks on my HUD. But they're moving. They're undulating closer like worms, and the sight of them brings the cold sickness back to my belly with a biting hunger.

I know exactly what they are. I know what they want, and in this place with so few memories of my own and a woman I barely trust, I have no idea how to stop them.

The Lag.

D. THE LAG

I watch them wriggling closer at maximum HUD resolution. Flare from the blazing purple star pulses across my visor like a heartbeat, but even through that coruscating distraction I can see that something is different. This Lag is not the same Lag I have fought a thousand times before.

It's space Lag.

"They're bigger," I say at last.

"Of course they look bigger," says Solfeje dismissively. "They're getting closer."

"That's not it. Do a rebound, calculate the distance and you'll see what I mean."

A moment passes.

"Ah," she murmurs quietly through blood-mic. "They're immense."

"They're damned tyrannosaurs. They could swallow this asteroid whole."

"You're right," she says, and turns to look at our asteroid. It's large, obviously bigger than the two ships inside it, but just one of those Lag worms could swallow it whole.

"We're dead," I say, reading the HUD display. "They're due in T-minus forty-seven minutes."

"Confirmed," says Solfeje. "The first wave at least, there's five of them in it."

I spin back and count them. Spread out like this they look like the wiggling aliens in a simplistic video game, with five in the first wave, eight in the next, then thirteen, and they're too small to see after that.

"Fibonacci numbers," I say. "Part of the golden spiral."

"Is that supposed to mean something?"

It's the kind of thing So would say and Ray would then question. I don't know why I said it. "I have no idea. It just means every wave is going to be exponentially bigger. They'll be unstoppable soon."

"Can we even stop this wave? How much amp has that shoulder cannon got?" She points back to the Bathyscaphe where I left it.

"A lot, but compared to them?" I think it through. "It might take one of them, maybe two. The QCs all focused together might take out another. That's three. After that, unless we can rig our sublavics to shoot plasma straight up at them, I think we need to be long gone by the time they arrive."

We both look toward the pulsing purple star.

"So all this is the Molten Core, and that's the Solid Core," Solfeje says. "It doesn't look too solid."

"It looks like it'll fry us to bacon."

She hums agreement, then points to my chest. "Hollow Star. Is that where you always write your mission objectives?"

INFILTRATE THE HOLLOW STAR

She's mocking me, and I grunt. I miss the others. "I didn't write that. Either way, we need to get off this rock. Can you think of any way to clear this distance and get us there?"

We both look across the massive orbital gulf to the sparking surface of the purple star.

"Not one," she says. "I've never been in space before."

"Neither have I. The screw on my ship wouldn't make any traction on a vacuum. My grapnels wouldn't get us one hundredth of the way to it. There's got to be some other way."

"Could we ride the Lag?"

I shake my head, even as I try to picture it. "I don't see how. We can't even kill them, how could we subdue one or hope to control it? They're too massive."

We both look around, thinking, but there is nothing here. We are just one floating rock in an orbital moat of floating rocks. There is no explosive powerful enough to launch us across the divide, no rope or umbilicus long enough to bridge it.

But that's the secondary problem. First we have to survive the first wave.

"We have to rig the ships," I say. "See if we can't align the plasma cannons to shoot the Lag down. That'll win us some time."

Solfeje nods smartly. "Agreed. But moving the ships will be impossible. Neither is designed for operation out of lava. What we should do is move the asteroid."

"What?"

"We can rotate it, I think. See that?" She points to one of the chunks of rock floating above us, just another part of the orbital belt. "I think I can grapnel over to it. From there, I go to," she weaves her finger through the air, settling on another larger rock a little further off, "that one. I drop a mass anchor using a QC and reset, and between us we should have enough elasteel to rig a pulley system."

I frown at her. "Are you suggesting we rotate the asteroid with pulleys?"

She nods firmly. "It shouldn't be so difficult. All the rocks are trapped in this gravity band, but their orientation isn't fixed. They'll rotate as easily as well-oiled artillery, with zero friction. One of us works the pulley while the other fine-tunes the aim."

I stare. "It's crazy."

"But it'll work, if you keep up your end."

"What's my end?"

"You stay with the ship and shoot them down. I'll set up the rig. I've got it all figured out already," she taps her HUD. "Better at math than targeting. How's your aim?"

"Solid."

"Good. If for some reason we can't align the ship in time, you've still got the shoulder cannon. You can take a few out before they hit, and maybe we'll get them all."

I run it through my mind. It seems technically possible. "OK."

"OK. So give me all your elasteel, I'll need it for the jump."

I don't hesitate to reel it out. "There's more in the other suits."

"Same for me," she says.

Without another word we drop down our grapnel lines and make for our respective ships to start harvesting elasteel. Between us we should be able to muster about ten clicks-worth. Given a distance of one click to the next rock over, that should allow a torque multiplier of five through the pulleys.

But is that enough?

Preparation takes fifteen minutes; I gather the scavenged elasteel and carry it to the sublavic top.

"Help me with these," Solfeje says, her helmeted head popping up from her conning tower ladderway. I jump over and she points down into the dim recesses of her ship, where a set of ten heavy-duty steel gearwheels lie. Pulleys.

"Where did you get them?" I ask.

"Salvaged the screw," she says. "QC on precision mode."

I admire the work. "We're almost ready, then. You need to start jumping."

"Agreed," she says. "There isn't much time."

T-minus twenty-six. On the outside of the asteroid I fire QC particles at the rock just enough to destabilize it to the texture of pudding, then work in two quadruple twined loops of elasteel for an anchor. When the rock re-sets they poke out like the wirework of a swept-away home.

"Done." I drop into the asteroid to find Solfeje looping her elasteel coils and pulleys. T-minus twenty. At T-minus fifteen Solfeje shoots a grapnel off to the other rock.

"Wish me luck," she says, then triggers her in-coil and zips off into the black, dragging her pulleys and ten clicks of looped elasteel after her.

Back in the Bathyscaphe I bring the front pulse cannons on line. Designed to cavitate lava and speed us through a Molten Core, they should make short work of the asteroid wall. I wire their sights through the periscope and fire, blowing a hole first through the brick hull then through the asteroid, revealing the empty black of space. Off the left side I can see one of the great Lag worms wriggling closer.

It makes me feel ill. I gag and channel shock-jacks just as a wave of something; nostalgia or sadness washes over me. I feel the absence of the others as a Soul-deep ache. I need them. I need Ray and Doe and La and…

I remember that Doe's dead. I always forget. But the others, they can't be dead, where are they?

"In position," comes Solfeje's voice, dragging me from this reverie. "Status report."

I blink and look at the controls before me, the gap. All of it feels so foreign. So should be doing this, not me. Still, I can read that the asteroid needs to turn by a yaw of some twenty degrees to bring the Lag into range. Then something occurs to me.

"Clear here," I call through blood-mic, "but how are we going to make the asteroid's rotation stop? If it over-rotates and I can't shoot all the Lag in one go…"

There's a long silence before she replies. It looks like neither of us thought of that. "We can't stop it. The pulleys can't brake. You'll just have to be sure to shoot them as you rotate past."

I try to imagine it. It seems near impossible. "So we have one shot at this."

"Multiple shots in a row," she confirms. "Excuse me while I bury this anchor."

The fizzling sound of her QC ripples through the comms. I shut down blood-mic and focus on the sights, playing with the degrees of range the pulse cannons have. It's not much. They're designed primarily for blunt forward thrust. This is going to be hard.

"T-minus ten," I call as the light in my HUD blinks

"The pulleys are set," Solfeje answers. "Everything looks good. Start the in-wind, slowly."

I fire up the conning tower's umblicus, designed for pulling an EVA suit through a Molten Core, and watch the elasteel pulley lines slowly tauten. Any moment the asteroid will start to turn. Through the hole I watch the Lag soaring closer, five asteroid-eating worms swimming through the blackness. Their mouths are black holes circled with dirty yellow fronds, trailing long whipping tails like spermatozoa, driving them on with all the grace of a convulsive fit.

I hate them. Far understands them maybe, but not me. I hate them because they take pieces of the chord and never give them back. Every loss bites into me and I want…

I don't know what I want.

T-minus six.

"The revolve's coming," Solfeje shouts on blood-mic. She's just barely visible from here on her rock; tiny and waving her arms. The lines are fully taut now, ten black elasteel ropes taking up the strain. "Get ready."

The kick hits; the asteroid jerks and I am knocked off my feet as the spin begins. After that it only gets faster, as the universe spins and the pulleys winch us around, bringing the sublavic's pulse cannons fast into alignment. T-minus five. The Lag's yellow mouths are almost on us, vast leeches as big as moons, and-

"On it." I lock into the periscope, scan out for the Lag and wait for the first of them to pass through the sweeping crosshairs of my trigger-sight.

VRRRRRP

I give it both barrels, bondless plasma jetting out in a hot blue stream that hits the first Lag full in its lipless dank mouth. Energy jitters across it spasmodically for a few seconds then it dissolves in a frothy burst of dust.

"One down," comes Solfeje's steady voice, "your window's creeping fast."

T-minus three until arrival, and she's right. I take aim at the next as my ship strafes swiftly across the black and hit it with both barrels again.

VRRRRRP

It dissociates just like the first. The asteroid tracks me across the sky and I take out the next before we even hit T-minus two, the fourth by T-minus one and I'm on course to finish the fifth with thirty seconds to spare, staring right into its champing jaws when-

SNAP

The asteroid kicks violently and I'm tossed backward as a massive soundless twang vibrates through the hull. I roll hard into the far wall and up to the ceiling as the asteroid enters a desperate spin. Something's gone wrong and now someone I don't know is shouting in my blood. Solfeje.

"The line snapped! The Lag's almost on you, Me. Get the shoulder cannon and blow it away."

"On it," I shout and try to get my feet under me, but it's hard to take a single step as the Bathyscaphe rolls like a spinning screw. I solve the problem by grapneling out through the conning tower and crab-clamping my way clear of the asteroid. T-minus twenty seconds and on the surface of the asteroid everything is spinning; the Star, the orbital belt, the Lag. I feel sick and dizzy and flush shock-jacks to steel me, settling my stomach and whirring mind.

The Lag is seconds away. Its huge yellow jaws spread wide, showing darkness and nothingness within; like the loss of my chord forever, a terror greater than any I can imagine. Somewhere far away I glimpse Solfeje firing her QCs across the distance but they're too weak and too distant, buffing only tiny gouges off the Lag's leviathan flank. I glimpse our pulley lines drifting loose in the interstellar void, surely sheared under the pressure, then I fire a QC clamp into the rock to hold me steady as the asteroid pirouettes, fire up Doe's accelerator cannon and wait for the rock to spin me into full alignment, T-minus two seconds, and fire.

Soul Killer

SLOOOOSH

The weapon unleashes a rush of gold-sheathed atoms that glitter across the sliver of void between us, impacting the Lag in its open yellow mouth, then it is upon me.

T-minus zero. Its great jaw closes over the asteroid even as it begins to dissolve from the inside out; its throat turns translucent as its innards backwash out and its jaw fragments into three parts. One chunk smashes into the asteroid near my feet, chewing out my clamp and sending me reeling into space, while the bulk of its body flows on to splatter across the asteroid in a flood of gray dissociated sludge.

"Solfeje!" I call through blood-mic as I hurtle away into space, trying to fire off a targeted grapnel but I'm spinning far too fast to get a lock. In seconds the centrifugal force overpowers my circulation and drives me into the dark.

ME

6. ASSAULT

The subthonic bursts through the desert crust like a Lag worm leaping from the mud of the Sunken World, and the jaw platform drops before it even comes to a stop, jolting us all as it hammers down onto the sand. Fresh salty air sucks in through the gap teeth, then the upper jaw winches back with a crunch of old gears to reveal a purple-black pre-dawn sky. I give the signal and our strike force revs out, hitting the sand hard and accelerating.

Wind rushes by as we tear down the wind-smoothed side of a dune, sand spitting up in our tracks and spraying off my suit like surf. I focus ahead; through the infra layer of my subthonic suit's Heads-Up-Display I search the rolling blank dark of coastal dunes, like an alien planet.

"Ahead of you, twenty-three degrees," So chimes.

I look out over the dark shoulders of sand to the flat Ohkotsk Sea, and see a structure jutting up through the horizon line that is eerily familiar, but completely out of place.

"It's a subglacic," comes Ray's voice through the bridge. He's supposed to be watching the skies around the suprarenes, but I'll allow him this. It is bizarre.

Through the infras I track the shape of the grounded boat, twisted on its port side at a dizzying angle on the Ohkotsk seashore as though it's been dropped there by the hand of a god.

"Almost," So says in my head. "Godship tsunami. It must've been carried all the way from the Arctic."

"By Goligh," Ray whispers, "and they're using it as a base?"

"Eyes on the skies," I tell him, while picking out some kind of radar array attached to the subglacic's periscope, bristling like kelp reeds rising from the shallows. "La, take out that radar array, but don't destroy the entrance."

"I'll clip it with a mortar," she says, and for a moment I'm looking through her eyes, down crosshairs in the Jeriko tank as she sights on the periscope, locks and fires.

The Jeriko jerks with the mortar-blast and I flip back to Me in the packed groundhog, surrounded by four men in my chord and five others controlled by Ti as the shell whines by overhead.

BADOOM

The ship's conning tower blows in a halogen-white flare through the infras. I flick to the eyes of one of my arenes with a better angle and watch the top of the subglacic burn; individual tongues of flame lick along the spikes of the radar array until it topples forward to the sand.

Hopefully now they're blind.

"Strafe pattern gamma," I call back to La as my groundhog tears on, the hot point of a spear with two wings following behind. I taste the air and drive the Warthog's engine harder. "Make them think it's a Dactyl attacking them; submerge the subthonic and keep moving."

"Already on it," she says.

"Movement!" Far calls through the bridge. "Something's happening on the bonds, I think it's a Lag."

I can sense it now too, through the grit in my face and the whine of another shell zipping overhead; the sense of an intense culling of memory happening ahead, just like at every Court so far. Hopefully we can make it before everything is erased.

La's second mortar explodes on the left of the subglacic, followed by a third in a strike pattern that should appear like overhead deployment. Geysers of shadowy dust plume into the sky chased by electric white crackles.

"Brace for ideation," I call across my arene-chord as our groundhog roars into the leaning shadow of the subglacic. Seven figures and I dismount, leaving two behind to drive the groundhogs to a safe and circling distance.

"Entrap," I shout, "La take the engines and I'll seize the con."

We break and circle around the still-burning radar array at a run, and I fire eight grapnel lines up the side of this tumbled behemoth with my eight bodies, then activate tracers to haul my selves up. I'm first over the rise onto the upper deck, feet on crumpled plate-metal, and train my HUD on the bombed conning tower.

There's a furrowed gouge canting inward to the interior con, all glowing hot on infras from the blast. Rifle fire peppers from within, striking sparks off the fragmented metal and one shot takes me in the thigh, penetrating the armadillo armor deeply enough to incapacitate me.

On one knee I snatch a mindbomb grenade from my shoulder bandolier with a smooth and practiced motion, yank the pin and hurl it into the gouge. I follow it immediately with my seven remaining hands, transferring my central consciousness to a new leader. We leap and climb into the mortar crater with our lines looped to the stub of the radar array; the lines catch and halt us at the edge of a heavily adapted conning tower, which I spray with Kaos shells even as-

BOOM

-the mindbomb grenade erupts ahead without any light or noise. Disruptive emptiness washes out and cores any Souls nearby, but I'm protected by the thump thump in my EMR helmets. Through infras I study the interior; some kind of mapping room, lined with banks of radar and sonar readouts. Three warm bodies lie on the deck by a green-glowing display screen; unhelmeted, unprepared, not brood members but hands.

I cut my lines, charge on and fire down the narrow corridor to the captain's hutch, eliciting another thud of flesh hitting metal. I hear muted BOOMS as more of La's mortars blow up the dunes around us, then the rest of my chord is with me. I loop our cables around the periscope glass then dive headfirst into the ladder leading down, two at a time in series.

An instant before the first pair of us hit the next deck head first the line slows us, and we unleash a hail of rifle fire down the dank corridor in both directions. One of me takes a bullet through the brain and dies, but another falls into place and keeps shooting, creating a beachhead for the rest to fall into.

We find out feet and our armor-piercing bullets ricochet crazily through this tin can. A rival hands fall in the darkness. A bullet thumps off my armadillo suit. I advance the chord and more bodies hit the deck in the darkness. With wordless commands I send my hands flooding in three different directions at once.

"Hurry, Me," Far calls, "whatever they're doing on the bonds is nearly finished."

I sprint down a narrow corridor chasing the sense of this ship-wide Lag. Into personal quarters I dive two more ladders, race down three corridors then blast my way through a wheel-locked bulkhead door with a TNT clamp into-

Not a dimly lit corridor nor a grease-marked deck of personal quarters but a tall and wide space completely decked out in white, with white lights, walls, machines, EMR and the sterile stink of CSF in the air, holding only two figures in the middle.

One of them is the skeletal remnant half of King Ruin, hanging limply on cords dug through her biceps and thighs with a thicket of cables rising from nodules in his spine. Where the front of his head was once attached to his long-dead twin I see the bulbous protuberance of a pulsing red brain, encased wrapped in transparent plastic. Old blood trails run down his sunken chest like water stains on the sublavic, ridged across his protruding ribs and sagging chest, meeting the trails running down from his thighs to pool in a broad black circle on the white floor.

It takes a second for my to recognize the pattern on the bonds; the Lag is happening to him. I pluck off my EMR helmet and throw it. It hits the ground by his feet and instantly expands in scope, cutting the King off from the Lag in a bubble as thick as the Wall.

The other figure turns to me. It's a man dressed in a white lab coat spattered with King Ruin's gray CSF and dark blood. His face bears the scars of deep gouges that look like they've been raked by fingernails, and the teeth in his smile have been filed down to sharp points, more like a shark than Mr. Ruin ever was.

My first thought is to reach out and Lag him, but he's protected by the bubble of my helmet now too, so instead I bead my Kaos rifle and shoot him in both knees.

"Don't move," I shout, advancing rapidly and three hands strong.

He doesn't even make a sound, just drops to the ground.

"It's you," he says, calm and smooth with a neo-Armorican accent, as though we're meeting in some genteel Calico coffee shop. "Ritry Goligh, the man who would be god. I wondered when we'd meet."

"Wonder on," I say, running closer with my rifle trained on his forehead. "Who the fuck are you?"

"Nobody," he says, then moves with an astonishing speed I hadn't thought possible with shot-out knees; lunging toward the King's frail body while palming a scalpel. I take off his hand with Kaos-fire before the blow falls, but it's close. Still he doesn't even shout as blood pumps from his ruptured wrist. I'm almost on him and can't read him at all; is he a brood member or a hand, or something else? I've never seen such pain tolerance before.

"Pain is so subjective," he says s if responding to my thoughts, then lunges the last few inches to sink his teeth into King Ruin's skeletal throat. I've already shot him fifteen times by the time his teeth touch flesh, but it's not enough. He jerks backward under the force of the bullets like a sail whipping in the wind, but the damage is done. King Ruin's neck, already thin as a chicken's with the spikes of his vertebrae jutting out, is pumping dark blood.

I send a hand to the King at once, injecting him with a brain-freezing engram that should crystalize his existing Molten Core before it fades any further, while simultaneously I advance on the man who did it. He twitches in a heap of his own innards and bone fragments, somehow still impossibly alive. He looks up at me with eyes full of blood driven there by the cavitation effect of Kaos ammunition at short range, and manages to speak.

"First time for everything," he says, then closes his eyes and sags.

"Goligh!"

I hear Far's shout just as the man dies, and on the heels of it comes a blast through the bridge like I've never felt before.

BOOM

I am dragged into its wake; a tsunami wave of power that blasts through the aether like a quakeseed just dropped, irrevocably altering everything in its path. I have to focus all my efforts just to maintain control of this hand.

Finally it's happened. I feel it just as every brood member in the world felt it when I was the first, standing atop my rollercoaster in CANDYLAND and throwing my life to the wind to take my final shot at Mr. Ruin.

This man just crashed through the aetheric bridge.

A second after he dies the whole hall erupts in ideation mines, and I am driven out of my hand as it crumples to the floor with the maddening pain, unable to do a thing as the pitiful figure of King Ruin shudders, shakes and dies.

7. KING RUIN

I jump into the last two bodies of my ten-member chord, the only ones outside the blast radius and propel them in to the subglacic and down to the white hall, past my twitching bodies while the aftermath of ideation backwashes off the walls like a frothy tide. I run one of them to the King and one to the man who just smashed through the bridge.

"Find him," I shout to Far as I lay one pair of hands on the King's pale, malformed head and the other on the blood-soaked assassin's forehead, hoping the skinship contact will help me get what I need. "Hunt him down!"

Then I jack in. The King is already fading under my touch, his unique Molten Core deeply corroded by first the Lag and now the ideation mines, but I pull out everything I can. There are thoughts in there still despite his death, partially preserved by the crystalizing engram I injected, but mostly he is garbled. I scalpel out what pieces I can and shunt them through the bridge to the others.

"So," I call, "Ti."

They descend on everything I find at once, and still I keep on pulling data until the King is empty and the only next step is to run his brain through augmented EMR for final pattern extraction.

At the same time I jack into the assassin, and recoil. Within I find a regimentation like I've never seen before. His mind is sectioned in rings of empty partitions as neat and perfect as the age-lines in a tree, layer over layer, with each one of them empty. His Solid Core is simple steel corridors and his Molten Core is barely lukewarm. He's like one of the King's hands but on a whole other order.

There is no sign of his Soul.

Not repressed or split in half, not curtailed or partially erased, just gone. I've never seen anything like it. It is alien and terrifying at once, and my thoughts reel around what this might mean. He died but he crashed through the bridge at the same time, leaving nothing at all behind.

I dig in through his Solid Core regardless, throwing open door after door to find everything scraped clean except one garbled load of data in what a kind of mental input space. It symbolizes as a towering pile of crumpled papers in a heaps in the middle of an otherwise empty room.

I approach and start uncrumpling, reading through pages written in other languages, pages of sketches, pages of random jottings that don't seem to make any sense, though a few words are repeated multiple times: my names. Ritry Goligh comes up, along with Doe, Ray, Far, So, La and Ti. It's about me. I search more papers and find Egyptian hieroglyphs, I find tallies of sacrifices, I find votive inscriptions.

It's knowledge taken from the King, about me, awaiting decryption.

I shudder and break contact, surfacing back into the white room with the King's dark blood running against my knee. This impossible assassin lies before me, shredded by bullets and missing his hand. He's not even human, but maybe he's something more at the same time.

Every time I passed through the bridge it was in pieces only. I never crashed my whole Soul through at once, and I don't know what the ramifications of that might be. I can't imagine what he's capable of now.

And he's hunting me.

I call the others to a conference at once, summoning the Dactyls and suprarenes to join me at this beached subglacic. We thought killing King Ruin would bring the war to a crashing end, but I see now that we were very wrong.

The war has just begun.

8. APOTHEOSIS

"We go after him," Far says. "We go now, we go hard and we rub him out completely."

We're standing on the Wall deck thirty minutes after the ideation mines blew, all the constituent parts of Ritry Goligh plus Yena. It's been a flurry of activity since the King died, with each of us making preparations, planning, jacking and throwing together theories.

"Where did he go, So?" I ask.

Her two-tiered map hovers as a holograph before us, again showing the purplish aether laid out over the Hollow Desert. Everywhere there are crisscrossing intersections as the two clash in new and unexpected ways.

"The blast wave he made by breaking open the bridge was massive," says So, starting a simulation that sends a flood of blue light out in every direction. Her voice is flatter than normal; in shock just like the rest of us. "It touched everything, but I've been able to follow the dregs of its wake to here." She points to one heavily massed locus in the aether, burning bright blue. "It corresponds to an Inuit city, Iqaluit, capital of their resurgent nation on the other side of the world, and a brood stronghold."

I rub my eyes. I've been looking at this map since I dragged the corpses of the King and his assassin out of the subglacic, and I still can't fully grasp what it means. Far knows, though, and he's staring hard waiting for me to see it too. But I have to be sure. I have to exhaust every possible avenue first.

I turn to Ray. "Can we raid Iqaluit by any conventional means?"

"No," he says swiftly. He doesn't wink or make some joke; none of us has energy to spare now. "The Dactyls couldn't get a quarter of the way there on their fuel tanks, let alone we'd be visible for a full day in the air if we could, overflying brood lands. Ti's subglacics could go secretly, but I'm not convinced we'll get anywhere near this bastard again in any kind of numbers; he's in the middle of a brood city."

I spin the floating map, studying the blazing blue locus and the many shifting correlations between it an Iqaluit. I run it backward in time to the point where the assassin died, then I run it forward again and watch the blast wave wash out across the aether. The force unleashed is phenomenal.

"Where did all this power come from?"

"From the Disjunct," says Far flatly, meeting my eyes and ushering me toward the inevitable conclusion. "It's the burst of power released when a Soul dies. It looks like that every time you die, just before I gather you back."

I frown. I've seen the Disjunct played out in simulations before; my Soul bursting out like a ripe seedpod to launch its patterns on the unseen aetheric wind. Far's been studying the Disjunct since we Became, jacking deeper every time to try and track where dying Souls go, but he hasn't found the destination yet.

"It's not like this when I die," I say. "I can't harness this kind of power. I'm just dead."

Far shakes his head. "We have harnessed it before; just not this efficiently. It's how Doe blew up half of King Ruin; she died. It's how I first leaped across the bridge to reach Mr. Ruin; I killed you, Doe and Ray. We used it explosively those times, destructively, really just surfing the wave unleashed from a fragment of a Soul passing on. But if we could harness it in this way, and from the death of a complete Soul..." He trails off.

I stare at him. I hadn't thought about that; it's true I am only one seventh of Ritry Goligh. So was Doe, and that was enough to half kill the King. "Harness it how?"

"I don't know, but we need to learn fast. With the Disunct as fuel, there's no telling what kind of power this man will have."

"He'll be unkillable," Ray chimes in. We all look at him. "Imagine it; right now Me can go in with a chord of ten and hop from mind to mind until they're all done, but when the last one dies he's sent back to wait for a few hours to overcome Disjunct and synchronize again. But if he could use that spike as fuel? He could hop into anyone, anywhere, without end. There'd be no way to stop him."

"Except I don't know how to do it," I say, "you're talking about this guy."

I point to the assassin's torn body lying behind us, his blood drying in the augmented EMR bay. King Ruin lies in another bay beside him, looking so wan and feeble I almost feel sorry for him.

"Who is he?" I ask, looking around my team. "Does anybody have anything?"

"Nothing," says Ti, "no bonds lead to him and none lead out, and there's nothing in his head but what we've all seen."

"Us," I say.

"Exactly. He was researching Ritry Goligh, pulling everything he could from King Ruin's mind. From the pattern of extensive damage in the King's Solid and Molten Cores I'd say he's been doing it since we half-killed him."

We all go quiet. It's no consolation to learn that the King has been tortured all this time. Instead it sends a thrill of fear shooting through me. In that muddled heap of papers I saw the six of us, with many details of our shared existence before Becoming. The assassin tortured it out of the King Ruin, who tortured it first out of Me.

Maybe this is how he learned to cross the bridge. Maybe he's been building to this moment since we Became, secretly marshaling the brood across the world.

It's an enemy we never even knew existed.

"So we can't kill him," Ray says, spelling it out, "and he's got all King Ruin's brood waiting at his call, desperate for a new leader. What's to stop him teaching them to jack the bridge too, wiping us out? What does that make him, then?"

Nobody answers. There is no answer.

"The new King," Ti says. Her hand has turned pale. "King of us all."

"More than that," I say, "he'll be a god."

Yena spins to me, anger on her face. She was always religious, and will take this as blasphemy. "What are you talking about?"

I turn to Far. I've heard him preparing through the bridge, setting in place a strategy I can't ignore. He takes a breath and says it. "Apotheosis."

Yena looks at him blankly.

"It's an ancient Greek word meaning 'ascension to godhood'," he goes on. "In my research I found ancient records that tell of a secret door into enormous power. The Greeks believed it could be entered through Avernus, the mouth into hell. The Vikings told of Yggdrasil, a giant nine-branched tree that reached into worlds beyond. The pharaohs of King Ruin's era believed in a hole through the sun god's eye which led into a timeless emptiness, from which any part of life could be altered. There are countless stories of those who walked through one of these doors and came back empowered."

"That could just be the bridge in the Solid Core," says Ray, though he doesn't sound so certain. "We do that every day."

"Perhaps," Far allows, "but I think there's something beyond that, a further bridge that leads beyond the aether to a place where all fates collide and all dead Souls return." He pauses. "I've been looking for it, and I think this brood-King is looking for it too. After harnessing his own Disjunct, maybe he's already found it."

This silences us all for a moment, until Ray grunts. "So you have to die to become a god?"

"In mythology, yes. It has to be total Soul-death though, not just a fragment. Only true self-sacrifice can lead to godhood."

Ti speaks up. "What would it even mean, to become a god? What could a god do that we can't?"

Far turns. "I can only imagine. Think about what we do every day, Ti. We speak to each other instantaneously across vast distances, we flit in and out of other bodies at will, able to kill with only a thought. We can't die either, as long as I'm there to catch us. So what can we not do? We can't change the past. We can't raise up a tsunami with a thought. Perhaps a god could do all of that."

Ray gives a low whistle.

"If such an inner bridge exists, we have to find it first."

I nod. This is one step we can take.

"We have to change," I say, taking command. "We don't have the luxury of time anymore; we have to go after this new King before he comes for us. Far?"

Far nods and picks up the thread, bringing up the map of Iquliat with the aether overlaid. He's been leading us here all along, and is about to begin the mission brief when Yena interrupts again. I can feel her emotions roiling on the bonds.

"How are you going to attack?"

Far looks at her. All the chord look at her. This is not her area and she knows it., but she doesn't care. "How? Me, I can see it in your eyes. Tell me how, when Ray said you can't get there any physical way. No Dactyls. No subglacics. So how?"

"Through the bridge," Far answers flatly. Making no excuses. "We core people in Iquliat and we use them as hands for an instant strike. It's the only way to take the brood-King out."

Silence falls for a moment as this sinks in like rain into dry sand. Yena's uncertainty hardens to anger. She looks to Far then back to me. "Is that true, Me? You're saying you intend to core innocents for this attack? It means killing them, you know that."

"We know it," Far says, "it's what we've-"

"Let him speak for himself," Yena snaps without looking. "Me, coring is what King Ruin did, and there's no going back from it. You're talking about mass murder. Tell me this is not your plan."

She must know from my face that it is.

"Innocents will die," Far answers for me. "You're right; we'll kill them and use them. It's terrible, it's something the old King would have done, but how else can we stop him? There is no other way. Would you rather millions become servants of an actual god?"

Yena rounds on Far, on us all. "You're talking about becoming gods yourselves! You're already acting like it. Me, I can't accept this. I forbid it."

She whirls back to me, all her love burning in her eyes. She went through such awful things in the glass menagerie, and for a time I was her savior, but I think not anymore. Maybe I don't deserve to be.

"It's already begun," I say. "I'm sorry, Yena. Far's already selected fifty target hands in Iquliat; solitary, lonely Souls whose loss won't cause too much pain to others. I don't see any other way."

Yena stares at me in disbelief for a long moment, then does something I hadn't expected. She slaps me. It cracks my head to the side, and the clapping sound of her open palm on my cheek rings out around the Wall deck. I turn back to see her finger stabbed at my face.

"You are not a god, Me!" she says with cold certainty in her voice. "You don't get to decide this. People are not your playthings, not pieces on a board you get to throw into any battle you want. This is not the way we win!"

"This is the only way we win," I say. "If you have another I want to hear it. What else can we do? Tell me, Yena, what else can we do?"

Her eyes blaze on mine, and I feel the bonds of love between us gradually burn away. We won't sleep together any more, I see that. We won't love anymore. It's too much. "Not this," she says. "I didn't fight for this, Me, for the war to be reduced to gods hurling people like ammunition at each other, using up the whole world to find a winner. It's not our war anymore, it's yours. You fight it out alone!"

"I would lose, Yena," I say softly. My cheek stings where she slapped me. "We would all lose. Do you think he'd be a fair and equitable god?"

"I don't want any god! Not him and not you. You don't get to decide for me. None of you fragments do!"

Her eyes shine with tears now and I feel King Ruin's menagerie uppermost in her thoughts, where every Soul was replaceable and instantly replaced. King Ruin kept them as entertainment and used them as fuel.

"It's not the same," I try to explain, "it's not because I want to, Yena, it's what has to be done."

She blinks the tears away and I feel the final cog in her mind turn against me. How could it be any other way? "So would you core Loralena? Would you core Art and Mem and use them as fuel if you had to? Or do they get special dispensation, the most favored of your toys?"

It stings worse than the slap. We've never talked about Loralena before. "That isn't fair. We won't core children or families-"

"So you get to judge!" she shouts. "You decide who gets to live or die?"

Now I give a gentle smile. This, then, is the difference, and why it has to be me. I never had a mother or a father, I was never wanted, and now I get to judge the whole of the world. I watch as Yena's beautiful, damaged Soul turns against me for it. She'll hate me now, and that is the last thing I want. I love her and I don't want this, but I'm powerless to change it. What kind of god would be so weak?

"I'm sorry," I say.

She almost starts to argue more, but I can feel her spirit cracking. It's a betrayal too far, showing me how deeply I have hurt her. Her eyes brim with tears as she sees me changing before her. I am the one on the path to godhood, after all, not her. I am the one who will choose who lives and who dies.

"Would you core me too?"

Now the tears come to my eyes. I owe her the truth, even as it comes to me in the moment. Once I've started dow this path, I can't stop at innocents. I can't stop at children or families or people I love. I have to take it to the end.

"Yes," I say, then Lag her intent before she can strike me again, and rage, and plead any longer. There is no time. The pain falls from her eyes and she wilts, caught gently by Ray.

She is just the first. I see I've run this war like a democracy for too long, and that has to change. I want nothing more than to hold Yena myself and take it all back, to apologize and say it's not who I really am, but it would do no good. It's said, it's done, and this is our world now.

9. YENA

We plan the strike for the morning, four hours away, and I send the chord to rest and prepare.

I cannot rest.

Yena breathes somewhere far off, in and out, steady as a metronome. I listen to her through many decks of the suprarene, like a voyeur. In sleep her anger is faded; she is the same bittersweet I fell in love with, though that is changing already.

I will miss her, when this is over. I already know she will never be mine again, and I commit to memory every detail of how this feels. I lie in the narrow alcove of my bed, where once she would have rested by my side, and let myself drift on the surface of her dreams.

They are not nightmares, but fantasies. Good things are happening inside her Molten Core, perhaps sparked by her freedom from me. Chimes tolling out with her mother's pulse spell healing and regrowth. I can only guess that rejecting me has led her to some deeper confidence and understanding. I could jack deeper into her mind and know for certain, see the images as her unconscious mind brings them to life and even insert myself into them, but I never would.

To lie here and drift on her deep-wave patterns is more than I have a right to. I think back on our nights of skinship, complex chemical exchanges taken for granted, indulging our body's hormones in a blur of healing. We brought comfort to each other through proximity for a time. It wasn't the horrors King Ruin created of oppressive, caged intimacy; all those bodies piled atop each other in skyscrapers and glass tombs and seaforts in Courts all around the world, slowly going mad.

It was something good. It helped teach us both that people are not the real horror. Bonds between people are what make us strong, not what destroy us. Now our bond is severed.

Rising from the surface of Yena's thoughts, I reach out further, taking the mood of the chord. Ray is asleep, and I have no problem peering into his dreams. Curiously they're not about sex, but about me and Doe. We're arguing about something; the words are indistinct so only the mime of it comes through.

Doe, so brilliant and so white, is shouting at me with her hands raised in fists. I'm shouting back. It's a disturbing image, one I'm tempted to Lag, but that's not for me to do. We agreed early on when we discovered the strange voyeurism of dreaming separate dreams we were all aware of, that while watching would be acceptable, intervention would not.

I let myself drift wider, untangling myself from the angry ghost-bonds of that dream argument, and envelop the suprarene tank with my thoughts. So is on the mapping floor, as always, and grunts in my direction. She's staring at her map as ever, hunting for better information. There are men and women on patrol on the suprarene top deck, looking out over the dunes. Further out, on the three tanks standing in diamond formation nearby, I feel the slow pattern of our hands in their bays, sleeping in unison without dreams.

La is below, her subthonic's screw paused just below the surface; a metal can enclosed in sand and shale. Ti is far off to the north, harbored underwater near Calico, taking on fuel and supplies in secret in preparation to assist our raid on Iquliat. Far, I can't feel. I reach into the bridge after him and find the track marks of his trail, but little more. He's jacking deep, searching again for the path to godhood.

I pull back, allowing this swirl of thoughts to suffuse me. A day ago I was plowing onward and now I am at a crossroads with only terrible options before me. Will I truly sacrifice innocents to bring down the brood-King? Will I truly lose Yena to achieve it?

The answer is yes, I already have.

I long to nestle closer to her, this strange, angry woman I have come to love. I imagine her hair in my face, smelling of desert orchids she must have gone out to fetch from rugged cacti on the desert floor. The flowers bloom once in twenty years, but she would always find them, some kind of reminder that she had control over her life and body. I think of an ancient history where Loralena once loved Ritry Goligh this way, loved our children this way, and wonder if this moment is the echo, or that was.

Thinking of ripples spreading in a pond that never ends, I sleep.

10. BROOD-KING

I wake to an explosion that floods the bonds. I lurch upright as further explosions erupt all around me, physical impacts that rock the suprarene itself and tell me everything I need to know.

We are under attack.

I flash to guards on patrol at the suprarene top, and through them see the night sky swarming with incoming craft. There are hundreds; all manner of helicopters hoving in low over the dune-line, their lights dark but the acrid flare of missile trails lighting up under their bellies.

"So, report," I call.

"I don't understand it, Me," she shouts back, "they crept up on us somehow." I hear chaos through her ears, see flashing red alarm lights everywhere across her map. "We didn't see them on radar, there was no warning."

More missiles explode on the suprarene's outer hull, sending violent quakes through the superstructure. I reach down to Yena, on her feet now and staring out of her angular porthole window with wide eyes, waiting for me to take command.

This is what I do.

"Ray," I call, sensing him already sprinting up to the helicopter deck, "get our Dactyls up and protect this tank. Ti take out all their craft that come anywhere near, I want the night sky lit up like a supernova. La, you're coming up right now, this instant, to the base of the last borehole, am I understood?"

I know that I am. I start running. At the same time I wake a dozen hands and start them running through the tank like ants in a hive, collecting every living Soul they can find and ushering them down.

"Far, where are you?" I call into the aether, but he's not there, not in Calico or any place this side of the bridge. I reach through the bridge and catch some trace of his passage, gone faint now with the depth, while at the same time I see the one thing that changed everything yesterday, repeated countless times.

The brood are jacking the bridge. Blast waves wash out everywhere I look; bursts of energy that mean we're too late. Their Souls swarm toward us directed by the new King's guiding hand, dozenss of them launched like missiles across the aether; rising up out of the Iquliat cluster, out of neo-Armorica, out of the Arctic fringe and proto-Rusk, from a hundred different points encircling us.

"They're everywhere, Me!" So shouts. "They're coming from everywhere."

The force of their bridge-dives crashes against my consciousness like a flurry of mindbombs, even as the first of them land against my golden shield within the aether, against So's and Ray's and everyone's, where they stab blades into their own hearts and explode.

Disjunct energy rocks out; unparalleled energy from suicide unleashes upon us, like the moment Doe killed King Ruin but repeated ten times, twenty, one hundred.

I stagger under the weight of it. Every blast against my golden shield shakes me more, and I realize this is the real attack. If anything the physical strike against our tanks is just a cover for this suicidal onslaught, like a rain of meteors flung through the darkness beyond the bridge.

"Help us!" I shout for Far into the aether, but no answer comes, then another missile blast yanks me back into the suprarene and descending stairs madly. I run half-clothed along a smoke-filled corridor until I come up to Yena, staring wild and filled with crippling terror.

"Me," she says, and I feel the glass menagerie foremost in her mind, the fear that she will be put back and tortured forever; I Lag the worst of it with what strength I can muster. I squeeze her arm so tight I know I'm bruising her and run with her back to the stairwell and down, metal-runged steps cutting welts into our bare feet.

More explosions rock the tank, there is the crackle of howitzer fire raking our hull and in the midst of it I send a hand racing sideways to fetch shoes. He meets us at the Wall deck where forty-seven minds remain, still locked into a protective cycle and shielding us on the bonds.

I grab the shoes and put them in Yena's hands. "Put these on and follow the hand," I tell her, while I start pulling soldiers out of the Wall in batches. They all deserve a chance to live.

"Me," says Yena, and I can see she's emerged from shock and can comprehend what's going on. She's been raided before, captured before, but still she's strong. "I'm sorry for what I said. I believe in you."

"I love you," I tell her, for the first time. "I won't let him take you. They won't take any of us again, I promise. Now run."

The weight of her love for me is almost more than I can bear. There's no time for a final kiss and no time to explain, there's only time to…

The first wave of ideation explosions strikes. I feel it as maddening pain in my hands readying to fight on deck, burning their nervous centers up in seconds. Through the eyes of a flagging soldier I watch as hormone bombs strapped with screaming bodies hurtle from the bellies of machines overhead to burst on metal. Clouds of poisonous chemicals bloom outward on impact, felling every Soul they touch with screaming agony.

The hand I'm watching through dies. I feel his pain and reel, because this is stronger than any ideation I've felt yet. I send orders out to So and La to close us up, seal every galley and hatch that can be sealed, but already it's too late, and seconds later I feel more hands dying in corridors and rooms within the suprarene. The hormones have filtered in through the fracture lines from the earlier blasts; they're inside here with us. We're none of us suited against it, none of us prepared for such a massive assault.

I push out with my mind, enveloping the Wall and Lagging away the suffering welling through my people and hands as best as I can, redoubling the command to flee. Far above I feel our guns coming online and see La hammering shells into the ranks of their buzzing helicopters as they descend on us like locusts. There must be a thousand brood-members out there swarming closer. I feel our Dactyls launch under Ray's guidance and start firing missiles, picking out the frontlines of this massed offensive.

From a last surviving hand on another suprarene's upper deck I watch the sky overhead fill with tracer-fire and urgent explosions, raining hormonic ideation on us and catching us unawares, rocking us on our massive treads with mortars and missiles that bite great chunks out of the armored walls, opening us to deeper infiltration. Black-clad marines with buzzing EMRs drop like a meteor storm on rappel lines.

I reach out further and faster, pulling deep from the chord's strength to Lag the ideation suffering as it lands, even as I drop into a vacant EMR and re-launch the Wall alone.

Blue light flares around the suprarene like a dome, augmented by my cleansing efforts against ideation. Ray and La spray the machines and marines in the air, establishing a temproary beachhead overhead, but there is no evading how immensely we are overwhelmed; our Dactyls rapidly flame out under incoming fire, our suprarene cannons gutter and erupt as mortars hit their munition banks, our hands drop one after another.

We have moments only.

I pull away from the fight and focus on the bonds, on keeping the ideation effects from slowing the flight out of the back of the suprarene and silently into the dark, toward the last bore-hole where any moment La will surface in her subthonic. I extend the umbrella of my protection out to them, in agony now as the massive forces I'm sucking out of the air threaten to tear my Soul apart.

It's too much, but there's no choice, and already he's here.

I feel the brood-King all around me, some kind of gestalt presence distributed through his many encircling marines, each tethered on tight bands of control. He's looking down through the aether like I'm an insect pinned under his boot, judging what I'm doing with distant curiosity, and in Far's absence taking aim.

I open my eyes in the aether and see him everywhere. He hangs across the universe like a sarcophagal shroud of black oil, only visible for the stars he occludes. There is a great spear held in his amorphous hand, the tip blazing hotter than King Ruin's Suns.

I can't defend myself at all, not if I hope to shield Yena and all the Souls fleeing under cover of the Wall across the dunes and into the dark night, away from the explosions and toward safety. In the aether my chest is wholly bared to this new figure, my golden shield already blown apart, and I can change none of it now.

"Far!" I shout. "Far, please!"

The first blow of his spear plunges into my chest with a crunch and pain like I've never felt before, because this is my Soul, not my body, impaled with a weapon I've never imagined. It passes through to core out of my back, and the pain buckles my consciousness and saps hard at my sense of self, making the Wall sputter and crack.

Screaming ideation bombs drop into those cracks in the real world, bursting in fogs of sand and gas that fell many of the Souls in their exodus trail. I gather myself and Lag their pain as best I can, then cry out as the spear sucks out of my chest, calling still for Far.

But he's gone, too far gone to ever come back.

CRUNCH

The spear strikes again, punching a second hole through which my Soul's blood flows into the aether. I have one terrible flash back to Doe dying in the depths of King Ruin supernova, dying forever, then the Wall slips out of my control.

Its blue light flickers out. In the sky above the suprarene the last of our Dactyls explode in spiraling flame, chopping themselves to shrapnel pieces as they fall under vast, orchestrated fire. I sense La racing between artillery emplacements seeking one that will still function, but they've all been destroyed. I sense Ti in the Arctic pinned down under her own attack; countless bombs dropping on the waters above her berth point and driving her down in a massive, globally synchronized attack. I feel So and Ray folding themselves through the bridge, only to stumble under the same aetheric onslaught that is killing me now.

Still I reach out, sheltering the last ten in the exodus from my suprarene, the last five, the last one, until Yena is running alone through the sand and the subthonic is surfacing just ahead.

So much has been lost already, all the others are dead, but as long as Yena survives then I have not lost everything, I have not failed everyone and I have not become the thing she feared most. I urge her on even as the shifting black figure drives its burning spear for a third time into my chest, this time pushing through my spectral ribs and cleaving my heart.

I gasp and break, and my shield over Yena falls. I can only watch through her own eyes as she drops to the sand, spasming with ideation pain that falls from the sky like rain, suffering again all the horrors I promised she never would.

"Far!" I scream as Yena contorts and screams. La's subthonic bursts through the surface just before her, but no arenes pour out to save those dying. They are not equipped for this and I cannot shield them now. They can do nothing.

"Yena," I whisper to her, striving with my last consciousness to Lag some of her pain. "I'm so sorry."

Through her eyes I watch as her last hope, the subthonic, sinks again out of sight. Missiles chase after it, sending gouts of sand and ruptured metal up into the air.

Soul Killer

So Yena dies. So La dies, and half a world away anti-subglacic mines boom all around Ti in a concerted onslaught until the subglacic is ruptured, the icy Arctic water floods, and Ti too dies.

I scream. Ray is gone, they're all gone, and my heart is broken. I am staring into the black depths of this new King that I cannot understand, that I don't know, that is killing me one strike at a time and can only think that he has already become a god.

"How?" I whisper, but no answer comes. I try to throw something back up at him but I have no strength left. I'm going to die for the fifth time but this time it's going to last, because I have wholly failed.

The spear crunches through me once more, burning a fourth sucking wound through my Soul, and at last the black figure speaks.

THANK YOU

-it says, its voice thrumming like thunder through the aetheric bonds.

THANK YOU FOR SHOWING ME THE WAY

I see everything I've done fritter away. I see in its black frame a world where every living Soul will disappear into a blackness so complete nothing will ever escape, at the hands of this newly minted god.

I sigh, I sob, because all of this I have done for nothing.

YOU HAVE DONE IT FOR ME

-answers the voice.

AGAIN, I THANK YOU

I'm fading, turning to a blur, and now this will be my legacy; that I unleashed this creature through the bridge and was unable to stop it, that all I ever did was play progenitor to demons in the form of gods.

"Far," I whisper weakly, "Far, please."
Then I go black. All the chord goes black with me. That is all.

--.

E. TRUST

I come to and I'm no longer spinning wildly through space, but I feel sick to the soles of my feet. Purple light flashes. I lean over and vomit; nothing comes. Two figures stand before me. Maybe it's one. Solfeje in her suit. I blink and she resolves then de-resolves.

"You're a lucky man, Me."

I laugh but it comes out wrong. I don't feel lucky. I feel like I'm close to vomiting myself to death, like Solmiz.

"You caught me," I say. My voice sounds hot and feverish. I need shock-jacks; I request them through my HUD but nothing comes. That's impossible. They can't be dry yet. I try to run a systems check but the suit seems to be shorted completely. Nothing works.

"You system's fried," Solfeje says. She kneels. We're on the asteroid surface, I think? It's hard to tell. I can't see much with the purple flare of the Hollow Star beaming down full in my face. "I barely brought you back around. It took all the shock-jacks you have. I'm worried you're not going to make it."

I feel another rush up my throat and hack out a few shattering coughs. Die like Solmiz, I think. I don't want to die like that.

"Can you spare some?"

She leans in and her visor fills my vision. It's opaque though and I can't see her face.

"Where's your other, Me?"

The question confuses me. I asked about shock-jacks. I become aware of a terrible stench and see gray dissociated Lag meat everywhere around me, lying on the asteroid's surface like a layer of rotting snow. It exploded from within, and even through the HUD I can smell it, like the putrefaction of a Sunken World.

Wait. What?

"I-" I begin, then stop. I can't remember what we were talking about. Did she ask about my chord? I'm too sick to think clearly.

"I went into your ship," Solfeje says, "after I rescued you. Trying to understand what you're looking for in the Hollow Star. Beyond the aetheric bridge."

I try and hold on to what she's saying, but the words roll off me like QC particles, constantly shifting their state. Do I know what the aetheric bridge is? I'm not sure. Maybe I do, but is it a secret I'm supposed to keep? I don't remember.

"I saw your forging pod. Seven pods, Me. You lied to me."

I see something in her visor now. I hear it through blood-mic. Anger.

"I-"

"Doe," she says, like an accusation, "Ray, Me, Far, So, La, Ti. Seven plaques on seven doors to seven rooms, Me. Seven notes in a chord."

I jaw at the air, trying to speak. All this seems very important but I can't quite grasp why. I feel half-forged again. I want to say that I saved us both and she can trust me because of that. The others are long dead and there's nothing to be afraid of, I'm alone like her, so what does it matter how many of me there once were?

"Tones," I manage to say, trying to come clean now. "Not notes."

She stares. Of course, I see I've betrayed her in this. She showed me Solmiz, half of her Soul dead in his pod, while I lied about the chord. Now I'm helpless. I need to do something, need to earn her trust back. Words spill out of me unplanned, not even really my story, but a story I know. "I never had a mother. I didn't hear a pulse. I only had the seven harmonic tones of my artificial womb. But I don't tell anyone that. I'm sorry I didn't tell you."

She stands up. She's a blur, as my eyes water. Then there is a QC pistol in my face.

"What?" I ask. I don't understand. "What are you doing?"

Her body starts to jerk. At first I don't know if I'm just imagining it, but it goes on; her arm twitching, her shoulders rolling, her legs buckling and kicking. It's some kind of fit. I can hear her teeth grating through blood-mic.

"Do you know who I am?" she asks through the fit, and her voice sounds choppy and strangled. "Do you even know what Solfeje means, Me?"

I gulp to speak. "It's your name."

She laughs, though through the convulsions her laughter is more of a guttural bark. Her arm holding the QC shakes. "It's a study," she says, "it means a study of the seven tones in a chord. And you're a chord."

"It's a good name," I say, casting out for something, anything. "A chord's a nice thing to study."

"It means I've studied you!" she gasps as the shaking becomes uncontrollable. "I know you."

She squeezes the trigger on her QC. I stare in horror. With the power dead the QC defenses of my suit will be minimal. A single QC particle could dissociate me completely.

"The Hollow Star," I blurt, "we said we'd go there together."

Her visor flashes up, and now I see her face. It's contorted. I see the sickness in her even as I feel it growing in me too. She's so pale. We should be helping each other. She wants me to see this.

"I know you now," she says. "I remember you. Me, of the chord."

A long moment passes, and the trembling steadily passes out of her body. It's an incredible act of will. I levy what control I can and try to do the same.

"How do you know me?" I ask.

"From another time. I know what you are and what you want, but I'm the one who'll get to decide, Me. I'm the one who'll take the Hollow Star and ascend to godhood."

I stare at her. I start to see things too, and remember things I didn't know before. I see trust, misplaced. We both lied. We were doomed from the start. We aren't here to help each other, but to win a terrible race. I see it all.

"You cut the pulley line," I say.

The accusation hangs between us. Her QC pistol doesn't waver. She stares.

"Why?"

"Because it has to be me."

"There's no way," I say, still clinging to the old frame. It's a better frame. I want it to be true. "We have to find a way together-"

"I found a way. On that other rock there's a ship that can fly the aether. It can carry two. It will only carry one. This is where your journey ends."

"I-"

"You shouldn't have trusted me, Ritry Goligh. I'm not a good man."

Soul Killer

She pulls the trigger and QC particles flood out and envelope me, rebounding off the suit at some points but working their way in at others, dissociating my flesh and bones to mush.

F. EVA

I remain conscious as my skin, my muscles, my sinews and tendons and bones and organs all dissolve to constituent matter beneath the antimatter touch of Solfeje's ricocheting QCs.

The sense of it is indescribable; not pain in any way I've ever felt before, as the particles do not damage the nerves that carry pain signals to my brain, they remove them completely. It feels like my body is being ground in a silent blender, with all sensation removed except the plain knowledge that it is happening.

It continues for long milliseconds as the QCs digest upward into my lungs and heart, burning themselves through my flesh until at last some emergency function in the suit reacts and clamps a triage sealing wall through my neck to shut them out.

CRUNCH

My spine shatters, and that hurts. I black out then come to flat and immobile in the dust, a jellyfish trapped in a dying helmet with flashing warnings in my HUD telling me that my whole body has just been amputated. The image from the mission pack flashes before my eyes again, the arch with Me and You written on the columns, and for a moment I glimpse something that seems very important.

I shout into blood-mic, barely gumming out a sound with no lungs left to project air. "We have to do it together, Solfeje. It's not too late."

"Quiet now," comes Solfeje's voice, then she breaks blood-mic contact and un-syncs our suits.

The image of pillars fades and I forget the clarity it brought. Now gray dust shivers on the surface of my visor as the QCs exhaust themselves within me, burring slight vibrations through my body. I request shock-jacks but of course nothing comes. I'm just a head kept alive by the suit, but...

It takes far too long to understand, seconds rather than milliseconds, but I grasp it at last. The suit was dead but now it's holding a bare sliver of power, registered at the edge of the HUD by a blinking red readout: T-minus five. The QCs must have charged the quantum battery through resonant harmony, buying me five minutes until the HUD's artificial heart and lungs die and I die along with them.

A lot can happen in a few minutes.

I subvocalize a string of commands to suture brain function directly to the suit's exo-motors, while ahead Solfeje grapnels across the aether to the surface of the pivot rock. On zoom I can see the ship she talked about; an ancient looking saucer-shaped craft no bigger than a few forging pods grafted together. She climbs in.

It has foils and a screw. As I watch she brings it online: the screw spins, the foils begin to blow dust and small rocks away, then the whole creaking, ancient thing lifts, hovers briefly then flies off the asteroid and away.

She's gone.

Revelations pile up in my lagging mind; that she saw this ship from the start and hid it from me, that her whole plan to rig pulleys was just a way to get over there without arousing my suspicion. She always expected the Lag to eat me. I was betrayed before we'd even begun.

Her craft picks up speed and soon I lose it in the stroboscopic flashing of the Star.

T-minus four minutes until total suit shutdown. I hope it's enough. I have the glimmer of a plan now; too reckless for anything other than a last-ditch hurrah.

Under rough jerry-rigged thought-control, the suit stands.

The exo-motors are imprecise. They're not designed to replace basic locomotive function. Normally they work to augment existing power, driving leaps and powering blows, but I can make them do this if I focus hard enough, if I work to consciously walk. I remember running dozens of hands at a time, in anoher life. I've jacked Souls with fresh memory engrams every day of my life; I think I can manage this.

The suit starts to run. It's shaky and it wobbles but soon picks up speed. The Lag meat underfoot is slick and the suit slips, but I factor that in. My grapnel is gone, taken by Solfeje, but it won't matter. At the hole we blasted through the asteroid's surface I drop. The suit fumbles the landing and I sprawl to the rock floor, hammering my face against the visor, but a broken nose is not much to me now.

I start to laugh; airless bites connected to no lungs. Maybe that's madness. At least there's nothing more to vomit, I think, and that cracks me up worse. A single leap carries me onto the brick back of the Bathyscaphe, and from there I drop into the conning tower.

T-minus three. I race down the corridor toward the captain's hutch, stopping halfway to pull one of the huge Extra Vehicular Activity concrete suits out on its rack.

This.

Where the combat suit is many-jointed and made of plates that can shift with full range of motion, the EVA suit has minimal jointing and minimal range of motion. It is closer to being a small sublavic itself, with its own rounded, bulky cement-clad hull.

There's a fresh message written for me on its chest in yellow paint.

CATCH SOLFEJE

I laugh more to see it. Is it really there or am I just seeing what I want to see? It doesn't matter; it sounds like a plan to me.

I unbolt the back and start stripping out all the internals I can, as the EVA rigs are not designed to fit a suit within a suit. T-minus two. I yank out the padding and bio-monitors, the haptic feedback and coolant arrays; all essential for a safe and comfortable ride, but I'm far beyond comfort now. T-minus one, and I feed my suit in. The exo-motors whine hard as leg-by-leg I force the sublavic suit in. Parts of it crumple under the pressure and tight confines, but I don't feel it. My nerve endings stop at the top of my spine now.

The countdown hits T-minus zero and the combat suit powers down, stops cleaning and oxygenating my meager amount of blood, but I re-route the last few milliseconds into a jolting pull.

In.

The EVA seals up around me, clamping into the socket at my throat and using its own power supply to charge me up.

The count resets.

I take a simulated breath. Shock-jacks wash in. By Goligh, that feels good. I'm veritably bouncing. I'm ready. My visor tells me that the next wave of the Lag is only a few minutes away from hitting. Solfeje must have been crawling over the Bathyscaphe for hours, but whatever, it doesn't matter now.

I take control of the EVA through the combat suit, a hand within a hand, and waddle it down the hutchway, scraping the metal walls to either side. I use the simple clamps it has in place of gloves to load its belly payload bay with concrete-clad candlebomb, then I tip its massive visor-less HUD-cap into position, encapsulating me inside and reducing my vision to only what the heat-shielded exterior camera sees.

I grapnel up onto the Bathyscaphe's back, where I fire a new accelerator cannon to strip back the asteroid's ceiling in slooshing clouds of bondless gold. Through the ship-long gap I can see the next rank of the Lag flicking desperately in toward the orbital ring.

One more adjustment.

My calculations are haphazard but the best chance I have. Out on the asteroid's surface, clomping along while the Lag champs nearer, I set candlebomb explosives in the right places. I've no time to rig another pulley system. I set the blasts to blood-mic control then descend. Within a minute I'm standing before the furnace doorway into the Molten Core, facing what I have to do alone.

I feel the heat already. The magma churns just feet away, held in by the gravity of its own mass; all fierce oranges, reds and yellows bubbling and twisting. I remember dropping La's body into magma much like this, a long long time ago.

I've never been so alone. I should have the chord with me for this, but they aren't here. There's nobody to tell, nobody to look at, nobody to share this moment with, and so be it. We'll find out soon; I expect I'll have just a few minutes.

I hook the umbilicus to the suit and push my stubby right arm into the lava flow; molten rock slides over the EVA concrete like liquid glass and draws me inward. I wonder if I will be able to get back out. I let it pull me in, folding into the blazing rock like an engram into a mind. Immediately the heat blows past intense; a few remnant coolants in the suit whine up to high-pitch to counteract it. Only liquid Freon cooling and a thick layer of plating lie between me and the burning heart of this asteroid.

Soon I am engulfed. Through the HUD's outer camera, in the moments before it melts, I watch the familiar chiaroscuro of a Molten Core. Willowy yellow sulfurs and manganese reds spin around thick revolving banks of darker ferro-carbon, each warp and weft a piece of the larger revolution. It feels like home. I channel suit power to the tail fins and propel inward.

The heat grows dizzying. My own sweat bathes me, collecting around my neckline and evaporating to fog within the visor. I swim on and soon the exterior camera burns away, leaving me to navigate by the suit's telemetry alone. It only gets hotter. The HUD counts down the estimated time I have left on the concrete cladding on the belly-bay, within which the candlebomb rests.

T-minus ten. T-minus nine.

The HUD tells me I've reached the asteroid's edge before I feel it through the suit's lagging haptics. Solid metal and molten rock feel much alike now. The magma flows push me against it, solid matter at the core. I have to hope.

I unclasp the candlebomb from its belly-bay and press it to the outer rock. The concrete cladding around it melts and bonds at once, holding it in position. It is the largest charge I could carry.

The umbilicus winds me in, and the flow back out is almost peaceful, though the heat is torturous. It becomes easy to ignore the blaring of my suit's warning light. I get so hot my vision grays, but this is what it takes so I do it.

How much time? T-minus three on the suit. T-minus five on the cladding.

I pour out of the Core like hot molasses and stagger away from the furnace as the cool vacuum air freezes the heat right off me, cracking the concrete suit's hull with loud pops. Single-use only.

I wrestle out of the EVA like an insect climbing from of a man-shaped chrysalis, exo-motors whining loud. T-minus three on the bombs? Residual charge from the EVA will keep my sublavic suit going for a few minutes after that. The Lag's here in four. I want to throw my head back and laugh out loud. If this, if that...

I lope back to the Bathyscaphe and leap down the chute into the conning tower, the HUD sloshing with sweat and vapor. I look up through the wide gash in the asteroid to the black mouths of Lag. T-minus one. They're so close now, eight ugly slugs kicking their inexorable way toward me.

I wave them goodbye. The countdown is down to seconds.

I fire the first rank of explosives placed on the asteroid's exterior, and the great rock responds with a terrifying jolt, throwing it into a spin. I wait and I watch, praying the vector is correct. The belt rotates by overhead and I fire the second rank.

The asteroid shifts track, pin-wheeling inward until the furrow I've cut in the roof is gliding toward an angle directly facing the Hollow Star. I set a fresh count and drop back into the Bathyscaphe.

Seconds on the Lag. Minutes on the suit. Down the corridor to the captain's hutch I bury myself among EVA suits and send the pulse to detonate the candlebomb deep in the Molten Core.

At first there is nothing, then there is a great and fiery heaving of the whole ship as the initial blast gases escape, then the rippling red glow from outside grows until the conning tower is bathed in it, until the corridor blazes red hot, until the light is so bright my HUD shuts off all visuals.

Then it erupts. The asteroid's Molten Core explodes with pent-up energy like a god's roar, lofting my ship like a child's ball atop a tsunami and punching it out through the opening in the asteroid's roof and into the gulf toward the Hollow Star on a volcanic geyser. I soar across the empty expanses toward the nimbus of pulsing purple light, and cry out with joy and ferocity despite my graying consciousness, because I'm on my way.

Solfeje tried to kill me, she left me behind, but I am Me of the chord and you should not fuck with me. Superheated lava pours into the Bathyscaphe through the open porthole, swaddling me like a baby, and wrapped up in solidifying rock I arc from this Chthonic Rock toward the Hollow Star on a pillar of molten fire.

I'm coming for you, Solfeje.

ME

11. ALONE

There's a hole, a deep black hole and I'm deep and black within it.

I think of King Ruin. Always I think first of King Ruin. He humiliated me, tortured and terrified me, stripped me down to nothing and in doing so helped make me what I am today.

In King Ruin's white chamber of horrors I learned truths that passed through the bridge to the rest of the chord, fundamentally changing who we are and who we Became. He taught us we are not our arms or legs, not our organs or skin, we are not our thoughts or ideas, we are not even only seven tones of a single Soul, but seven constituent Souls combined within a greater gestalt being.

Ritry Goligh.

I surface from the darkness filled with dread and memory. My eyes open in a terrible, familiar space; not the gray of Far's Reach hideout or the orange sand of the Hollow Desert, but a place I never thought I'd return to, buried in rock.

A hissing halogen lamp illuminates bare rock walls and a ceiling spray-coated with cracked cement. Saltwater drips through the gaps, leaving crystalized stalactites of salt hanging down. Bolted to the gloomy walls are racks of cages, empty now but for the straggling bones and leathery skin of King Ruin's dead experiments. Beneath them are rows of cracked vats, some still filled with glutinous dark liquid. In one a chunk of unrecognizable pale flesh floats on the surface, lit from below by a low and glowering halogen-flicker.

The bonds hum with the hangover tang of familiar cored pain. It's an experimental Court.

Spartan's Crag.

The sense of dread redoubles, and I remember that my chord are dead. I gasp as this understanding deepens like a third-degree burn. It wasn't a dream. They're really all dead and I am somehow alive, somehow here.

How? Why?

I rise to my feet in a rough triangle of light cast by three halogen lamps set around me. Dripping water plinks off old metal. The lull and shush of the Arctic Ocean breathes far above.

"Far," I whisper, my voice a croak. It hurts to speak. "Ray."

No answer comes.

I reach out to the bonds but of course this place is empty, scrubbed clean after Ritry Goligh once Lagged it for strength. I can't feel the chord because they're all dead, and that absence sears like I've had my whole body amputated. Still I strain for some connection in vain, but I can't feel anything, not the chord or the brood-King or poor dead Yena or…

I reach wider and feel some kind of EMR Wall hemming me in.

"Far," I call again louder, hoping against reality that he'll be there, because I need him to be.

I rise to my feet and peer into the shadows, past corroded metal tables and workbenches where once innocent victims were sawn into pieces in the name of crossing the bridge, but none of the chord are there, hiding. I feel like I've been forged into the Bathyscaphe alone. My head throbs like it never has after Disjunct. Five times, now, I have died.

"Somebody," I call but no answer comes, only a flat wet echo. "Far!"

I look down at the arms and legs of this new body, and see my clothes are filthy and marred with some astringent-smelling black substance, like tar or motor oil. I pull up the sleeves of my black cloth jacket to see grazes and dark bruises spreading over the skin of my pale forearms. I never woke from death so weary and battered.

What has this hand been doing?

I reach for the bridge seeking answers trailing back, but it is closed to me. I reach around its edges, in the inner space of my Solid Core where the blast door handle should be, but there is no handle at all. I cannot budge it reach through to the aether. I can't feel anything beyond this body or this rock at all.

I start running, as if I can outrun the truth. Through the jumbled pathways of stirrupped metal benches I go, past strewn electric cables, catheter-like ducting and assorted rusted saw blades and meathooks where once a hundred grotesque experiments hung. I run toward the exit and charge up the winding tunnel by the light of a few staggered lanterns. My legs throb with every step, as though I've already been running for hours, but I continue on, tumbling off the walls like a pinball. I pass up through a guard's room where half-decomposed bodies lie in their uniforms still, with Kaos rifles and key-fobs sinking into their leatherized skin, and up, until fresh cold Arctic air hits me and I burst out into gray.

I slip at the rock's wet edge and almost fall, barely catching my balance on a rusted railing. All around me lies the Arctic Ocean, rough and choppy under a strong wind. Overhead fierce gray clouds tumble like the Lag, threatening a deluge. I spin in wild circles, my eyes alighting on the ring of sea-forts, their brown leg pillars marked out by white wave-froth, just as they were when I last came this way.

There is no one here. The only sign of life is a speedboat moored below, lapping harshly against rubber tires hung from the Crag's shabby dock. It too is empty, bar a few lengths of frayed blue rope and a single can of pineapples rocking on its side with the waves.

"Far!" I shout. "Ray, So, Ti, where are you?"

Still no answer comes. A moment later the deluge begins, falling on me like an endless spray of freezing surf, but I have nowhere else to go.

"Far!" I yell into the rain until I am hoarse, until my clothes are drenched through and my shivering is so strong I worry I may tremble off the Crag and into the water. In this beaten, bedraggled condition, I'm not sure I could even climb back up.

The chord are gone.

I retreat. I walk shuddering back down the rocky stairs along with a stream of rainwater, and for the first time notice the low thrum of pumps. The Crag is at least operational, and I will not drown.

I stop at one of the halogens set along the descending corridor and touch it, as if this contact will give me some answers. It is a cold light that offers no comfort. I move on, feeling numb. I stop in the guard's room and remember the day I first came through here and shot them all, back when I was still Ritry Goligh.

I see now that they were playing a game of cards. Their poker hands still lie on the table where they fell. I notice one of them has a full house, aces and nines.

I feel disembodied, standing here in my own decaying trail. Time has hollowed me out. I am not Ritry Goligh anymore, full of seven nascent Souls, I am only Me and this is a dead, Lagged Court from a different man's past.

I feel like laughing. This is a ruin of my own life, and I am its King. I'm delirious and dangerously exhausted. What I really need now, I think, is some vodka. The laughter breaks out of my throat in a weird shuddery bark. Ritry Goligh would drink, and curse, and get into fights. But I'm Me, I've always had the chord and responsibilities, except now I don't.

I remember dying in the aether. How am I even alive?

I head back down to the hall where I woke up; it is empty still. The EMR shield still buzzes, but I can sense something through it now: the Soul-trail left by this hand, in the hours before I was birthed into it. I track it back and forth, unloading the speedboat to carry the contents down here, and I begin to understand.

This was Far.

At one edge of the dripping hall I find a pile of plastic crates tucked underneath a surgery table. I squat and pick through the contents: one crate loaded with bottled water, another with tinned goods, one with clothes and another with weapons and combat gear. In one crate there is a sleeping bag, a tent, and several canisters of gas for the halogen lamps. In the penultimate I find a sheaf of scribbled notes in a red binder, and beneath that lies an EMR helmet; it is switched on and throwing up a Wall that blocks my access to the bonds. My first reaction is to turn it off, but words are painted across its top in thick yellow paint.

LEAVE IT ON, ME

I leave it on. I slump to sit on the cold rock floor with the helmet at my side and the binder in my hands, feeling the chill reaching up from the core of the earth. The binder is a mission pack. It says those words on the front page.

MISSION PACK

I can't think clearly now; I need to be told what to do. I turn the first page, noticing there are blotches of ink on my own fingers that seem to match the ridges and whorls of fingerprints on the paper. I wrote this, it seems. I can feel this hand's trail upon it. Far wrote it through this body, before he made way for me.

A block of text faces me and I start to read.

Do not turn the EMR off, Me. When you leave this place take the

Soul Killer

helmet with you. The brood-King will find you the instant you turn it off. For now he thinks you're dead, but if he catches even the faintest glimmer of you, he will come and it will be over.

HE HAS THE BRIDGE, ME. HE HAS THE BONDS. DO NOT ATTEMPT TO JACK BEYOND THIS EMR SHELL.

While he was raiding the suprarenes and the subglacics and the subthonic, I was in the aether. I went deeper than I've ever been before, and saw things I've never seen, but I did not find the inner bridge to godhood. I still don't even know if it exists.

I only know you have to find it.

I heard you calling, Me. I came back, but I was too late and you were all dead. The King came for me too, but with the last of my strength I brought you here. It was the only way, with the bridge so completely colonized.

DO NOT TRY TO CROSS THE BRIDGE.

If you do this, you will only do it once. He is everywhere there and the aether belongs to him now. I barely slipped through. By the time you read this I will be gone.

You are alone now like you never were before. I know this will be hard, but you must remember that Loralena is still alive. Our children are still alive.

You have to kill him, Me. I don't know how or if that's even possible anymore. He is more powerful than King Ruin ever was, and already far along the path toward godhood. There is no telling what he will do with that power.

You have to become a god first, Me, whatever it takes. You have to make sacrifices.

I'm sorry I couldn't save more of us. I'm sorry I can't be there with you now.

Don't turn off the EMR. Don't cross the bridge. Thank you for being our captain, Me, and giving us all a place to belong.

Far

P.S. I left what you need in the final crate. Think of me fondly, please.

I can't really see for the tears in my eyes, but I pull the final crate over. It clinks as it moves. I pull off the lid and look in.

Subglacic vodka. There must be ten bottles.

I start to sob, wildly and out of control. I can't see, am a teary mess, but there's no one here to see me and I don't care. There'll be no one to see me ever again.

I wrench the cap off the nearest bottle, bring it to my mouth and glug it down. The cold vodka stings in my mouth and burns down my throat, and I gulp it like milk from the mother I never had. I was alone then and I'm alone now, and this is what I need more than anything. This is the only salve for the wound of losing the last five parts of my broken Soul.

I am no captain anymore. I am no father, no husband, there is no hope for me to be Ritry Goligh again. I have become Napoleon, alone and abandoned at a monster's whim, and I have lost everything.

I'm sorry, I moan into the bottle. Far, I'm sorry.

I drink until I can't drink anymore.

12. MY CAPTAIN

I vomit throughout the night, because in this body I have never drunk before. I shiver and shake, because it's cold and the halogens give off no heat. By the morning I have drunk down two of the vodka bottles and five of the fifteen water bottles Far left me with, and thrown them all back up.

Now I lie curled on the stone floor, half-wrapped in a sleeping bag, vomiting only occasionally. It's too hard to get up and go to a corner. This is not my home so I don't care.

Alcohol is not good for me, but I can't die any more, which was always my addiction, so this is what I have. The day comes up and goes by, changing nothing in this dripping, dark laboratory grave. I moan my way through the hours. A million fears and regrets pass through my head. In the afternoon I stir enough to open a can and eat.

As the day turns to evening I begin to come out of the fog. It's amazing how quickly the mind can grow used to something. I still feel Yena's death and the death of the chord, but now they're dead and it's over, and there's work to be done.

By the light of the halogens I take up Far's MISSION PACK and read.

BLACK SEA MONASTERY

You need to know who he is to defeat him, Me. He broke us with such ease because he knew us so well. Just as Mr. Ruin's knowledge blew open King Ruin's golden shield, you need to learn who the brood-King is.

There is a school on the Black Sea, off Turkey. It is an old monastery on a cliff-edge, where King Ruin took his brood-children for training. Perhaps there will be something there to help.

Here are the coordinates. I wish you luck, my captain.

Far

36.759385, 28.235251

I sit back. I remember the monastery as a brief blip borrowed through shared-chord memory, when Doe was watching the film inside Mr. Ruin's White Tower. The teacher was a skinned corpse lecturing to bored-looking children.

King Ruin's brood.

Perhaps the brood-King was raised there. Perhaps it might be enough.

I look at his signature for a time, so simple and clean. He was always so intense. I don't think he ever thought of his addiction to the aether as an addiction. It was his duty and he did it; like So at her radar, like La in the sand, like Ray keeping the morale of all our people together.

I glance through the rest of the mission pack. There are some roughly sketched maps of the Black Sea coastline and monastery, of the layout of Iquliat and where the new King might be, of the Hollow Desert and the circle we had once cleared within it.

I put the papers down and crawl to the food cart to open a can of meatballs in gravy. I try not to think of what a god might say if he or she saw me now, sucking at my fingers with old vomit on my sleeves.

13. NEWLY FORGED

The next morning I feel clear. The confusion, fear and grief of the days before have gone, leaving only a solid core of certainty behind. There are things I must do, and that is why I'm now alive. It feels as though the liquor has burned the doubt out of me, boiling me down to crystal.

I am Me, and this is my mission.

A warm breeze blows into this stale rock, smelling of hot dust, salt, and hydrate froth. I get to my feet and strip off my filthy clothes, crusty with vomit and engine oil. My new body underneath is pale, like Ritry Goligh, an Arctic breed. The bruises and grazes I saw when I woke, from hauling all these crates out of the speedboat, are beginning to fade.

I feel newly forged.

I walk naked up the winding cavern stairs, past the dead guards and glowing halogens, out into a world full of light. The sky is a furious blue, the sun is gloriously warm, almost as if I was back in the desert. The Arctic gets such days maybe once a year, usually in the wake of a typhoon.

I look to the speedboat, and luckily it is still there. Without that I'd truly be stranded.

I dive from the Crag, into the ocean. It is cold and bracing and wonderful. I wonder, when did I last swim like this? There is no water in the Darain, bar a few pitiful oases, most of which were infected with Courts. Every place we went had been corrupted.

Not here. This place is clean again, after Ritry Goligh Lagged it a year or so past. I see fish squirling away from me, into their cubbyholes in the underwater slopes of the Crag. I swim forward with powerful strokes, luxuriating in the feel of the water on my skin.

The salt tingles as it touches my grazes, but it is a good pain, a healing pain.

I reach the first sea fort without really aiming for it. I climb up into it, my new toes clinging to the metal rungs like barnacles, following a path I once took with armed men at my back. I sidle past the Bofors gun, rusted-stiff, and edge around the side to the entrance.

Inside the fort there are bodies, but not a hint of suffering. I almost cry to see this. Here are the dead, but they are clean. Their pain is long gone, and I did this. I have done good things.

It doesn't matter that I am naked. I am only another person, like them. I stalk inside and gather the first of them up. He is a boy, mummified, his skin crisp like fried pigskin. He saw such terrors in here, but the horror now is gone. Now this place is just another coffin.

I carry him to the edge, then drop him carefully into the water below, where he sinks. His constituent matter will rejoin the world, and the fish will feed. This is a good thing.

There are hundreds more in the first fort alone. It takes all day to clear them, and I do it until my back aches and my legs throb. I could push them out in great batches, as many of them have shrunk down to sticks and leather like the carved dolls in Mr. Ruin's Sunken World pyramid, but I do not. I gather them one by one, and let them drop one by one.

No one will ever know I have done this. These Souls are at rest already. But a god does not do things just so other people can see.

It takes two days more to empty all the forts. I eat the food Far brought with me. I drink the water. I look at the vodka and smile. Last of all, I enter the hydrate mine, suspended above the Arctic like the sea forts. It is no different from the others, only in how the bodies have been stored. There are dozens stuffed in the fuel tank, where they must have drowned. There are dozens dropped in the screw shafts, where they were chopped into fragments when the screws were turned on. There are hundreds lying in every possible position, stacked and folded, heaped and hung.

I drop them all into the water. I cleanse this Court for a final time.

Standing on top of the mine's uppermost cab, holding to an antennae array, I feel an upswell of pride as I look out over these lost, forgotten buildings. It is the first Court I have truly cleansed, in both body and bonds. It is a new domain from which I will build. Standing here like this, it does not seem so impossible that I might become a god.

Back in the Crag I put on the arene suit and the EMR-thumping HUD. The noise fades away quickly, canceled by buffers in the helmet. The suit itself fits well, just as well as any of the combat suits I wore on assaults into Darain Courts.

I flick the switch on the EMR in the crate, and its low thump powers down. Inside the Crag there is only silence. I reach out carefully through the bonds, feeling the limits of the micro-Wall thrown out by my helmet EMR. It expands about as wide as the walls of the room, and no further. It is a pillar of invisibility, and it will follow me everywhere. Perhaps with this, I can do enough.

I Lag the bonds made by my passage over the past several days. Nobody will know I was ever here, except me. I gather up the crates, mostly empty now, and carry them to the crag top, where I place a few in the speedboat and drop the rest into the ocean. They bob away, carried by the waves. It is gray today, and a cold and dusty wind blows from the north. The ocean rolls heavily, and the clouds foretell rain.

I'm ready. I look around a final time, at the forts and mine and Crag, then I drop into the boat, untether it from the makeshift harbor, gun the engine to life, and tear away over the water.

--.

G. THE WAR

The pillar of magma rockets me across the aether. The Bathyscaphe's hull shudders beneath the incredible heat and pressure, and curled amongst the smoking EVA suits I watch the metal ceiling strip away to reveal the frenzied purple surface of the Hollow Star beyond, zooming closer like an accelerator blast. Fire plumes around the ship's ruptured brick cladding like a thorny crown, and just as the count on my HUD's power supply clicks over to zero a blinding purple light envelops me and I open my eyes to-

Gray.

There are gray walls and gray floors around me, studded with pipes and rivets that thrum with the familiar burr of a screw turning far below. There's the smell of Cerebro-Spinal Fluid vodka and sweat in the air, and ice and blood, and…

I blink, suffused with a dizzying mix of memory and sensation. I'm in a Soul-jack station. There's a large thumping EMR machine in front of me with a marine lying on the input tray, and somehow I remember this. The marine's some kid who lost both his eyes in a raid back in the thick of the War, and I taught him to see again. Ritry Goligh taught him to see, that is. I look down, too confused by the dislocation to really question it; he's already had his implants, rudimentary eyes that will do the work of vision and talk to his brain, but as I remember, he doesn't want them.

Souls are fragile, I think, as I look into his unseeing new eyes. Old thoughts supersede new ones; how I felt the first time I performed this jack. He's too angry and lost to accept the implants, still running the maze of the hydrate mine where he was injured, and he doesn't want my help; he doesn't want to be fixed. Of course, this is not his choice, not in the War, not when his nation needs him to fight.

Soul Killer

It's just one of a thousand jacks that I made, that Ritry Goligh made, and I lean into it now like a dream version of myself, moving through the motions my gestalt self made a long time ago. I jack into the marine's Soul and I flow through his Molten Core as a chord in the Bathyscaphe, split unconsciously into a sub-split of Doe, Ray, Me, Far, So, La and Ti, changing his brain so that he'll work. I pluck at the threads that build his resistance, the emotions and scar tissue the Soul thinks it needs to keep him safe, and I pull them away. This is not even healing, but rewriting. I erase the memories that hold him back and remake him as the marine we need him to be. I fix him, and now he'll never be the same, because of Me.

The War always came first, and Ritry served the War, and I served Ritry. Whatever mission he needed, I led the chord to complete. For this and so many other crimes I'll be paying reparations for the rest of my life.

When the jack is done the marines looks up at me through his new eyes for the first time, a different man. I remember how this felt; always a heady cocktail of emotions at the cutting edge of the Soul, with our mutual survival mattering most of all. I remember that there is no room for softness and only the smallest room for compassion, because anything else will kill us all. I know this so well, because it was Ritry's softness that killed Ven and all his crew.

My crew.

The marine stands and nods his thanks. His hand uncurls from within mine, though I hadn't realized I was holding it. My hand, not Ritry Goligh's, but what is the difference in this place? Dark recognition pours through me; what have I just done here, but an early kind of coring? I Lagged swathes of what this young man is. He is now a 'hand' for the War, a slave to the mission, just another body slain on the ice.

Time slips around me like a night in the Skulks. I come back to myself sitting in the jack-bay in the aftermath with Heclan, drinking the strongest CSF he brewed and trying to rub the memory of what we have done away.

"We helped him," Heclan says, slurring his words and sloshing his liquor. The door is barred and it is just the two of us now, turning ourselves into fuzzy copies of ourselves to get us through the worst. "He'll live better. He'll survive harder."

"We changed him," I slur back with no real resistance in my words, only misery at having to accept them. "We broke him."

Heclan burps and swigs his CSF. "Fuck this War," he says, and I clink jars with him.

"Fuck this War," I agree, a constant refrain.

This was one day, I think, as I feel the liquor roll down my throat; a precious memory of a time so long ago, of friends and lovers that I lost. I want to be here so much I can't express it in words; trapped like a passenger in this old version of Ritry Goligh. I was never really clean, but I was cleanest here. I was better, still innocent of my greatest crimes. Every day I was with people I loved, and everything seemed so real while we were in it together, suffering together, fighting together, before I was alone.

I breathe in the moment and the loss. I suck it up and time slips again.

Now I am here.

Lying on my back, I gaze up at the metal ceiling. I feel indescribably happy. I roll over and see a woman who looks like Doe looking back at me, lying in our shitty little bed in her shitty captain's room, before any of it went wrong. Her face is so pale, her eyes so clear of conscience, and it is everything I can do not to weep. She is here. She is beside me, and I haven't yet caused her and them all to die.

Ven.

I am really back in the War, where I belong.

ME

14. RACHRANIKA

In a day I reach Calico. The boat is running on fumes by then, choking out as I pull close to the proto-Calico verge of floating barges. The Skulks. I've never seen them with my own eyes before, Me, this fragment of Ritry Goligh. For him it was reality, a pit in which he grew out of the chrysalis of his survivor's guilt.

To me it is a distant memory, a black and white history that lived long before I was born.

The tsunami Wall rises off-white above the Skulks like a vast and sheltering hand. One day this too will be crushed by the ravages of time. Looking at all this I remember Ritry's life, lived on both sides of that wall. On one there was despair, on the other, hope. I know what lies beyond; Loralena and the children, and also what lies beneath; Don Zachary's broken bunker.

I let my eyes fall across the ramshackle line of the Skulks, all-new since Ritry destroyed them with a quakeseed a year ago, but already stretching as far as I can see to either side. Neon lights pick out their conjoined contours; the bars, brothels and barrios that make these lawless, forsaken neighborhoods tick, that keep the flow of money flowing through. They seem in places to hover magically over the dark water, buoyed atop a low blue line.

These are the barrels that keep the proto-city afloat. Atop them lies a foundation-structure of twisted rebar and driftwood salvaged from the last Skulks, with reclaimed blue-tarp matting and plate-metal hewn from the gutted innards of old subglacics. The Skulks are a forager's world, last bastion of traumatized marines and all those who can't face the structure, law and forward-looking hope of Calico.

The engine sputters and I coax it a little farther, to the place where a great black ash-stain rears up the side of the wall like a towering

Rorschach blot. I flip the EMR HUD's visor down and zoom in, picking out the pit-marks and freshly-poured cement reinforcements stippling the wall's black face.

This is what my quakeseed wrought. Ritry Goligh's quakeseed. It did not destroy Calico, and I'm grateful. It did not tear down the wall, beyond which the family of my other life lies, but everything else…

Below the scorch-marks lies just another Skulk, agglomerated buildings made of flotsam, freshly built atop the bunker that once stood here. I spot a bar at the water's edge, its neon light flashing a tawdry Morse welcome into the evening dark, regular as a lighthouse.

ZACHARY'S

Someone has a sense of humor, perhaps.

I throttle the boat up to the mooring clamps of this replacement Skulk, already looking for my next mode of transport. I can't get to the Black Sea in a speedboat. I need something faster and larger.

I climb from the boat onto a bobbing jetty strewn with drying gray seaweed and octopus skins, their smell of salty desiccation rising up in a fog. I take only Far's mission pack with me, pressed close to my chest in a plastic wallet. Before me a narrow alley lies open, lined with scraggy metal facades that were once boat-hulls and welded metal container doors. I walk into it like I was born here. Here in the midst of the neon Skulks I taste the old familiar stink of desperation and lust.

The barrels of this floating world loll and bob underfoot as I pad inward. I can feel the trails of other Souls moving around me, within the aegis of the EMR helmet. They crawl in and out of lean-to buildings and shabby flotsam huts like silkworms boring holes in leaves. Everybody's seeking something. I stand in the midst of them and feel the change on the air already.

The brood-King is draining the bonds. It is faint here, distant, but I can detect the sapping on every living thing, pulling life out of them on thin tendrils; fish-hooked into their Souls and stealing a portion of their strength like an invisible tithe.

This was always King Ruin's dream, to shave the whole of the aether through the bridge. Now it's happening. The people don't feel it, they don't see it, but their lives are gradually being emptied out. I can reach no further than the bubble around me, not beyond the wall of my HUD's shielding EMR, but I can imagine their Soul-trails lines sucking up through the bridge in every direction, in every part of the world.

The power of them must be immense. Is it enough to become a god?

Somebody laughs from a second-floor window to my right, and I look up. Purplish smoke and the scent of old liquor wafts outward. A swarthy red-faced man leans on the rusted sill looking down at me, a leering grin on his face.

"War's twenty years over pal," he calls, pointing at my helmet. "What you wearing that for?"

He is within my EMR shield and I read his thoughts with ease; a proto-Rusk on a freighter run from the great hydrate dust-bowl out east. There is a prostitute in the next room he longs to have sex with, but he's already dreading looking into her face and seeing the fakery. He's planning to look away at just that moment, so it can seem more real.

He'll suffice. I reach out to either side and feel many more Souls, some of them his fellow crew, some of them the prostitutes, barmen and masseuses that will cater to their wants. They are exactly the people I am here to save, and exactly the kind of people I need.

Sacrifices, Far wrote in the pack. I am ready for this now.

With a thought, I core them. All consciousness fades from their heads. I erase them in a blink and send their Souls spiking into the aether. If anyone across the bridge should notice, they will probably think it's just more Don-wannabes cleaning house.

But who would care?

It is awful, but I can't think about that. This is a Soul-jack to save us all, as Far reminded me. I cannot be weak anymore.

I reach into these new hands. At my call they come out from their rat-warrens of lean-to acrylic and ruptured boat-hulls; junkies and dealers, whores and hustlers and johns. There are almost forty of them, the largest chord I have yet controlled; dressed in ragged lingerie, in oil-stained canvas freighter-wear, in the pressed seaweed cloth that passes for summer clothes here. They are young and old, men and women, all fragile loners looking for something.

It's awful, how easy it is.

We move together like a lava flow up the narrow alleyways of this Skulk. In the shadow of the tsunami wall we head along the walkway toward the mid-Skulk off-load pumps. Perhaps a hundred freighter ships are moored there, surrounded by gantries and jetties and the towering hollow horse-frames of loading cranes.

We walk into it; this gap in the Skulks like a cankered open mouth that serves to feed Calico's fuel and food needs. Hundreds of smaller boats bob between the giant tankers like nesting crulls, from tiny fishing junks with reams of net to whale harvesters, their decks stained black with rendered blubber-soot and blood.

The raucous cries of drunk freighters beset us as we pass, asking if we are some kind of parade. "Are you a guru?" One of them asks me, staggering near. "I always wanted a guru."

I Lag only his memory of me. I have enough hands for now.

We pass through makeshift markets, where despite the late hour Skulk-workers are tramping their feet in large plastic paddling pools filled with whale blubber, grinding it to paste for packaging in old tin cans. We pass down interwoven alleyways where all manner of misshapen fish, manta rays and sharks hang to dry like cast-off clothes. I smell salt and fish blood and the grimy tang of rotting sawdust, used to pack whale meat into crates.

I Lag all memory of us as we pass, until we reach the proto-Rusk's freighter.

RACHRANIKA

From the Molten Core of one of my new chord, an engineer, I learn this name is a portmanteau meaning 'early spring'. It is beautiful. The ship is not, a towering wall of flaking red paint and rust, laden down with perhaps two hundred long metal shipping canisters, only half-unloaded. These will be carrying Arctic hydrates, probably unrefined, and highly explosive.

This whole ship is a bomb. I can smell the nitric stink of the hydrates in the air, which taking me back to the War.

We climb into the ship. I send those already on board back out and Lag them of the memory of it. They will wonder where their ship has gone, shortly. I ascend to the captain's bridge, in a forecastle two stories above deck. It is not like a subglacic at all, and there is no periscope, only windows. I have never captained a ship this size before, but it is not so hard now that I have access to the memories of all these freightermen and women. They already know their roles.

We ease out of our berth without commotion. At some point a man on dock waves a red flag at us, but it doesn't concern me. He is too far away to Lag, outside of my Wall. This kind of piracy happens all the time. I have stolen their goods, and perhaps they will commission a war party to follow me. That would not be so bad. If they send military hardware in my wake, even better.

I'd like a helicopter, a Dactyl if they have any. I'm too far away to place the order on the bonds. I'll find one if I need it.

Flanking engines steadily turn us until we face the open ocean. The route ahead is long and arced, bringing us down around the sunken hub of old Europa to the Black Sea. At full speed I estimate it will take seven days.

I need seven days to prepare. I sit back in the captain's chair, behind the polished rosewood wheel. I have just killed forty people, forty votive sacrifices, but I can't think about that now. I am on my way to becoming a god.

I order food from the kitchens. My EMR Wall is large enough to encompass most of the ship, so I can control my hands most of the time. I put the ex-junkies to work peeling potatoes and the ex-whores to work grilling old whale meat. It'll be a welcome feast.

15. RAGE

We glide over the ocean; down the jagged curves of proto-Rusk, around the bomb-shelled coastline of Europe, all vast lakes and upheaved coral beds, and circle the great horn of Portugal. From there we cross the Mediterranean, where the thick salt water buoys us tall.

We pass other tankers, steamers, whalers, fishing fleets. A crop of pirate junks pass us by in the second night, eleven men and three slave women below decks, hungering for some shallow kind of conquest. I Lag the men absently, leaving the women in control of their own fate.

We pass up the Bosporus causeway, once a strait but now a wide channel cleared by years of tsunami. Few others pass this way, as the Black Sea basin is now a morphological wasteland. There is only sand, and dust, and no rain falls.

Three days pass. I work my crew, my new batch of hands, and when the work is done I shut them down. At times they all sleep, while I walk the decks and halls of this vast tanker alone. In the belly I tap the hydrate tanks and listen to the dull echo of the condensed fuel sloshing like the tides. In the outdated Soul-jack room I roll flasks of CSF in my hands, sitting in the EMR-chair and thinking about the future. In the large canteen amidships I sit amongst my hands like a King, while they lie unconscious about me like snakes, sunning themselves.

I wonder at the temptations King Ruin felt at such power, at how easy it was for him/her to do the things he did, once he/she'd taken that first step. Sitting there surrounded by these unfeeling bodies, I measure the distance between myself and such deeds.

It is not so great, and that surprises me. One different choice and I might have become the predator Mr. Ruin wanted me to be. I am glad that there is no appeal in such cruelties for me. Even if I enjoyed them they would still be self-harm, slitting my own Soul along with theirs just to feel something, when I feel plenty already.

I feel rage.

For three days I take the air and I plan. Standing on top of the containers, these faded red, blue and green metal boxes rising ten stories tall off the deck, I look out to the Hollow Desert far to the south and east. Out there lies the remnant of my army, in smoking, ideation-broken ruin. Out there lies a subglacic with a Lagged Court in it, and a shattered suprarene with the dregs of King Ruin. Out there lies Ray, and So, and La and Yena.

The air is different here. I can taste it in the wind, blowing sultry and salty over my skin. The sand smells of desolation. On the Arctic it is sadness, tinged enough with a human touch that there is emotion attached still. Here there is not even that. This is a world reclaimed a long time past, taken from us by the sand, the wind, the dust.

I reach out within the EMR bubble that walls me in and feel the death of the bonds accelerate. The brood-King is drawing more power. I can feel him faintly at the border of the Wall, like a black hole sucking everything in. His fish-hook lines have become a flood, a tsunami flowing toward Iquliat. He is surely building something there, a tower large enough to jack through even the deepest bridge.

Sitting in the captain's open cabin, my hand resting on the Engine Order Telegraph lever while the ship hums and buzzes with cleaning, cooking, eating and shitting like an ant farm below, I think about why.

Why.

I could go to Iquliat, I could raise an army large enough to fill my bubble and I could try to fight, but against the power that he has? It would be like trying to fight the magnetic pole with iron filings. He has the direct route to every Soul, and all I have is this pillar of silence filled with sacrificed slaves that do my bidding. I wonder if it would be worth it if I core half the world, and he cores the other half, so that we could fight.

Yena saw this coming.

I think back to what Far wrote about him, and wonder what he wants. I felt him in the aether, and there was no joy in the moment he killed me. He isn't angry and vengeful like King Ruin. He isn't lonely and lost like Mr. Ruin. I remember the feel of his mind in mine, as he thanked me.

At the time it felt like gloating, a final twist of the spear, but now I see it wasn't intended to be cruel. It was sincere. The brood-King wanted to thank me for helping him to kill my world, for helping him become a god.

Perhaps all the times I died really did help him. Perhaps he saw something in those deaths that not even Far could see.

I look over Far's notes again, riffling in the dry wind, though already I've memorized every word. If I cross the bridge it can only be once, but the bridge is the only possible path to becoming a god, so at some point I must cross it.

Now the brood-King stands guard. To pass through, I must pass through him.

How long do I have? I do not know. Ten days have passed since he raided my army. His draw on the world grows stronger and his apotheosis could come at any moment. There is no more time for delay.

So, we arrive.

16. MONASTERY

The monastery is as I remember it from Mr. Ruin's memories, displayed for Doe on a projector screen in the White Tower. It is set into a sheer white limestone cliff, above which lies a blue sky and below which surge deep blue breakers.

The monastery complex hugs the cliff some five hundred feet up; three interconnected structures with open-face cloisters poised near the top, arched out of travertine lime and dressed with faded veiny marble. There is no telling how deeply they press into the rock. They stretch half as long as my tanker, rising to a large circular tower like a conning tower atop a sharp jut of cliff, capped with light red terracotta slates.

It is from within that circular turret, in one of many classrooms given over to lessons, that Mr. Ruin's projector-screen memory comes. There he listened to the lecturing corpse of a skinned cadaver along with all the King's brood, dreaming of the day he would do worse deeds himself and earn his father's pride.

Even from here I can feel the residue they have left in the bonds, like rat poison. Thousands have passed through here, all children found in Courts who survived one way or another and became his brood. Every one of the brood I have met and killed in the Hollow Desert, in Saunderston, on the Arctic waters passed through this place at some point.

The tanker grinds closer, scratching its hull on rocks in the shallow water, and I reach for some sign of the brood-King. If all the brood came this way, leaving their bond-lines stretching away in every direction, then so did he; but I don't feel him. I would know him, I feel his signature on the wind as he drains us all, but he is not here.

There is no trace.

Standing at the base of the cliff, my tanker close to foundering on the dark red sandstone crags jutting through the water, I look up at the monastery. It is suspended on stone trellises emerging from the cliff, like a barnacle clinging to life. I can feel from the bonds that it has clung here for over a thousand years, populated for most of that time by ancient men and women of some long-dead god, who came to this remote, inhospitable place searching for some kind of meaning.

I feel them strongly, beneath the thick cladding of muck the brood have laid over them like shit and straw on a stable's solid flagstones. Here hundreds of holy seekers once lived in cenobitic, communal perfection, each one an experiment in how humans might best exist.

Scattered about the cliff-face I pick out the pockmarks of their tiny shallow caves, each one a cell that once held anchorite hermits; those whose faith was so strong they sought to live only for prayer, confining themselves to a solitary life for decades at a time. In their tiny self-imposed culverts in the rock, they ate what food and water was passed down by their brethren, each one a mind steeping in its own juices and living full in the face of god. Some of them even had themselves immured, bricked-in to their cells, with only the tiniest slit through which they could see the world without and receive their sustenance.

I look out over the sky and ocean and wonder where their god is now. Is it me? Were they waiting for me, or the brood-King? I wonder what they saw in all this blue that made their strange and lonely lives worthwhile, that prevented them from hurling themselves out of their cells to die on the rocks below.

Meet your maker, my darlings, meet the one who made you.

The echoes of their minds are alien to me. As for the killings and the torture of the brood that lie above them like sedimentary clay, that I am used to; I have lived through, I have seen a thousand times before. But this faith, the same glory I felt in the battered godships, stymies me and defies all explanation. What they did seems to have no meaning but at once has all the meaning I can imagine. They thought for us all. Their minds ran calculations that informed everything that came after.

Even these thoughts confuse me. I feel they come from without, involving ideas I did not initiate; that leap and tumble free of logic or the laws I understand. Perhaps something Far saw in the depths has altered me. Perhaps he learned something after all.

Still there is no sign of the brood-King.

The tanker halts, drops anchor, and we climb. Grapnels would help but we have none, so we gather rope and begin the ascent by hand, ten of my chord and me operating as one organism, all arms and legs propelling us upward. For climbing stays we use bolt guns from the tanker's engine-room, fixing a pinball-pattern of nails into this ancient cliff-face. As I climb, controlling twenty arms and twenty legs beyond my own, I imagine a great metal ball tumbling down and striking off these tiny pins we have left behind, scoring points before splashing massively into the ocean.

Halfway up we come upon a ladder carved into the rock, its stone rungs worn slippery and shiny with a thousand years of climbing. The rungs simply begin at a point in the middle of the cliff, below which there are no more. Perhaps this was the work of the monks above, to climb up and down ceaselessly. Perhaps when their time came they simply climbed down and dropped off the bottom, and that was their end.

We climb it like ants along a trail of honey, still shooting bolts into the rock for safety. I have only this body now, and this one EMR helmet that traps me within it. I cannot afford to lose either.

The ladder leads into a small cell cantilevered out from the main cloister and we emerge within it, into a cool room blackened with old blood. In single file we emerge through the opening in the floor, and I catch glimpses of the varied ways King Ruin's initiates would eviscerate their subjects here.

I shut them off. Deeper back in time I see the monks passing through this space, painstakingly chiseling the ladder's rungs out of stone.

From the cell we enter into a long stone-ribbed cloister hall. To the left is the cliff-face and to the right are open walls held up with thick columns, providing a balcony on an amazing view of the blue Black Sea.

We walk on; five of my hands ahead, five behind. Now there are numerous archways carved into the raw rock on the left, their wooden doors long rotted to dust, each leading into small cells. Sunlight floods into each, illuminating the dried-up husks of mummified bodies on the floor. A few still hang pinned to the walls where they were left by the brood, but most have crumbled to the floor and lie in the dust of ancient desks, beds and scrolls.

I lean in to one cell and rub the dust between my fingers. I can feel its history through the bonds, a compost of memories like my tower of memory in Candyland: a dissolved holy script one man spent a lifetime etching with gold, desiccated lice eggs, rough-wool blankets, human skin and bone, the many tortures the brood brought in latter days.

It has no smell or special sense. It is dust only, like all the dust of the world, but even in it I can feel the fishhooks of the brood-King. This too he is drawing on and thinning out.

We move on. At the end of the first cloister a stone bridge carries us to the next. Here the wall on the right is limited to slitted windows in the lime and the ceiling vaults upward like a cathedral, half built of stone blocks, half carved into the cliff, though the line where one gives over to the other is unclear. The craftsmanship is unadorned but startling in its perfect fusion. I see on the floor the marks where long mahogany pews imported from Africa once stood, the pulpit where the abbot once gave sermons. The central aisle is marked by a wide, shallow channel in the stone where ages of penitent feet have worn it away.

There is a sense of old reverence here still which even the debaucheries of the brood have been unable to remove. I see more of their nails stippling the walls, where they strung up their victims to practice a mockery of ancient religious figures, but they could not touch the deep communal Soul of the place; that sense of endless striving for something pure and holy despite the pains and pangs of the flesh.

"He didn't Lag it," I say.

My own voice startles me. I haven't spoken aloud for a week.

"He didn't Lag it," I say again, enjoying the way my new mouth vibrates and the way the sound echoes in that chamber. My hands pay no attention.

I wonder at this odd choice by King Ruin. To have left the ancient memories of this place intact means he let his brood grow up around them. Perhaps he saw it as a perverse reminder of everything they would stand against. Perhaps it amused him. Perhaps it was another form of torture.

I no longer know what I'm looking for, with no hint of the brood-King here, but I continue regardless. We exit the cathedral and pass through a complex of other huddled stone buildings: a small rock church hanging on a trellis, a kitchen with stone ovens, a library thick with the dust of old books, a dormitory for the lowest-ranked monks stretching back into the rock, a small iron forge, a stone font with water trickling down from a channeled slit in the cliff, a brew house, and finally the rounded tower at the peak.

Stone stairs turn in a circle from the tower's base, and I climb them with my chord of hands trailing behind. We pass by small open windows in the stone wall through which I catch glimpses of the ocean, graced by small puffs of sea air. After five revolutions I emerge into an open landing off which two rooms diverge.

Classrooms. I step into the first and it is like stepping into the past. The view through the stone window is the same as in Mr. Ruin's memory. The front wall and chalkboard are here still; there are even several skeletons of past lecturers laid out by the front desk.

"Attention, class," I find myself saying.

Of course the room is empty, though I can feel the potential of what it once held. I can see the bond-lines of a hundred generations of brood-members stretching out into the world. Some of them are vaguely familiar, perhaps ones that I have already killed.

Is there a hint of him here?

I walk to the desk that was once Mr. Ruin's. It is still here, stained dark with blood like all the desks. My ten hands stand in the doorway watching me blindly, and I send them back. This is not for them.

I sit.

Mr. Ruin once sat here as a child. I jack into the bonds held within this space, of an infant gathered from between his dead mother's legs and raised in the madness of this place. Fellow brood-members became his mother and father, King Ruin was his god and this was his world. There were no friends here, there was no love, no affection, only a single mission.

Make the King proud.

All his childhood he was tormented in inventive ways that only seasoned torturers could know. He continued the cycle of abuse as soon as he was large enough to; he had to or he would die. Those who were cruelest, who could make themselves most feared, survived. The others did not.

It is of course sad, but I am done with sympathy for Mr. Ruin and the brood. The infants they once were died when King Ruin took them, and they became my enemy. If I could reach out and kill them all at a stroke, I would, with no remorse.

I open the little desk but there is nothing inside bar dust. I feel Mr. Ruin's recent tracks through this space, only several years past. He must have come here in the years I was living with my family in Calico, waiting for his crop to come to fruition. He came to suck what little sustenance he could from the memory of past glories.

I stand. This place is empty. It has been a wasted trip, and the brood-King has left no trail I can follow, which means there is no trail I can conceivably find.

So I go to Iquliat, to muster as much of an assault as I can.

I push back through my chord. My footsteps slap loudly down the spiral stairs and back through the warren of buildings into the cathedral. I am halfway down the nave when I finally sense it, reaching tentatively out toward me within my EMR Wall.

A Soul.

It is gone in a second, like a dead satellite twinkling in the sunlight as it revolves, but the pattern it leaves behind is clear and I cling to it.

The brood-King.

It is not him, not by a long distance, but there is a deep, abiding, all-consuming terror of him here. There is one who knows him. I snatch out, reaching to the outer edge of my EMR Wall and find the Soul to which this fear belongs, immured within solid rock at the end of a bricked-in passageway, long-mad and haunted by terror.

It knows him.

My chord floods into every dark hole in the rock to root this lost Soul out.

--.

J. STRANGE

"You look strange," Ven says, studying me from inches away on her shitty bed in her tiny, shitty hutch of a room. "What's wrong with your eyes?"

I blink, barely keeping the tears from flowing, and slide up onto on elbow. I rush my hand up to my eyes and rub them. I can't believe this.

"I'm fine," I say, "something got in my eye."

She's looking at me still, doubtful. "While you were sleeping?"

Her face is a blur and I rub at my eyes more. I want to give her a massive hug and cover her cold white face in kisses, but I don't think she'd like that.

"Probably a spider," I manage. "Your ship is full of them."

She snorts. "I killed all the spiders on this ship myself. There are none."

For a moment I have the image of Ven; expression intent, cheeks daubed with blue warpaint, holding a burning torch in one hand and a spear in the other, hunting spiders through the subglacic's narrow halls. I laugh.

She frowns, perhaps guessing the image she's given me. By that I can judge this is many months into our time together, after she'd started to soften and adapt to being around another person so intimately.

"I gassed them," she says. "Before we embarked. The whole ship was decontaminated for rats, cockroaches, fleas, everything. It couldn't possibly be a spider."

Now I do lean in and kiss her. Her confusion delights me. I kiss her on the other cheek, pushing the moment as far as I can.

"Stop it," she commands. "I don't have time to do this again."

"There's always time," I say, pulling back the covers to reveal her pale naked chest, breasts squashed up between her arms. It shocks me how easily I slip back into the horny young man Ritry Goligh once was.

"Perhaps for an alcoholic Soul Jacker," she says, batting my hand off the cover and rolling sideways from the bed. "Not for the ship's commander."

I lie like a louche on her sad little bed, watching while she gets up and pulls a fresh and crisp uniform off one of a dozen hangers slung from a gray pipe. She starts to put it on, an unreal sight that I drink in. Ven who I was never right for, never good for, who changed me forever.

I bite my thumb to see if this is real, and it hurts.

"What are you doing now?" she ask.

"I'm hungry," I say, right back into teasing again. There's the frown again and I love it. She doesn't know if I'm serious or not. Probably she's about to suggest I go to the communal mess. I catch some faint sense of that in the air but she withholds, still uncertain if I'm teasing or not and opting to get on with dressing herself.

I lay back and watch. She is slimmer than I remember, her cheeks more angular, her breasts tauter and smaller, and I can even see the outline of her ribs beneath her skin, but she is Ven still. I never had any photographs from this time; only the rough, bruised memories I sheltered of her through the long EMR Lag, after the mindbomb fell.

What matters is not her body though but the Soul lodged inside, like a pearl in a gnarly shell. That is more beautiful, more innocent, more hesitantly loving than any I had ever known until then. With her, for the first time, I no longer felt like a freak.

Thinking these thoughts while she gets dressed makes tears spring to my eyes again. She's looking at me again.

"It is not a spider," she accuses, and this just delights me further. I would leap to my feet and gather her up in my arms, but I've done enough of that already. Ven was always like a cat, willful and independent, and she never welcomed unforeseen affection. It's enough that I kissed her twice outside the ritual movements of sex.

"It's your beauty," I say goofily, as goofy as anything I said in my early twenties, when I was packed full of shallow self-confidence papered over chasms of insecurity. "It's blinding me."

"You are strange this morning. You should rise too. We have the circuit of Iquliat to run, and there are many marines that need the appropriate skillsets."

I nod dumbly, surprised by the name of the place. Iquliat. It sounds familiar, and that jolts me somehow. Where am I really, I wonder? On a purple Hollow Star after crossing from an orbital ring of asteroids after Solfeje betrayed me, or in a neo-Armorican subglacic working my way through the War, or am I dead and this is what happens when you die, or maybe some combination of all three? Am I Me, or Ritry Goligh, or some combination of those two?

"Ritry," she says, answering the question for appearances' sake at least. "Get up and go jack my marines."

I wipe my eyes with my forearm and rise. I am naked too, and the chill off the ship's bare metal walls strikes me like an Arctic breeze. I remember briefly a year spent in a blue-tarp park on the Skulks, eyeing a fellow marine across the way, living with blood and bruises and always subject to the weather.

Ven is watching me

I shake it off and cast about for my clothes. There'll be time to figure things out later. "Where are-" I mumble, but Ven cuts me off.

"I threw them in the incinerator, as they stank of alcohol. I don't know where you get it, I destroyed all the alcohol on board this ship too."

I remember this; a faint recollection of this exact moment, along with another image of her stalking the corridors in her cavewoman paint, digging out cowering bottles of booze. I must have hidden this memory so deeply I even forgot it, sheltered like a tiny spark in my mind. I even remember what I said the last time.

"Then give me a bra," I say, following the script laid out some twenty-five years ago. "And some panties, a thong will be fine. I'll go collect new clothes at the commissary."

Her mouth opens wide, scandalized. "I don't have a thong. And you may not take my bra!"

I get up nonchalantly and go over to the brown wooden chest of drawers against the wall, the only hint of anything natural in this room, and start riffling through her underwear. "This one maybe," I say, tossing a scarlet bra I bought for her on one of our offshore breaks onto the bed behind me. I toss the matching scarlet panties. "Maybe these?"

"No!" she hisses, as though afraid someone will hear us. She is at my side now, closing the drawer and grabbing at my hands. "You wear your uniform; there's one spare in the cupboard."

"These look a lot more attractive, I think I can pull them off

She covers my mouth with her hand. "I am the captain," she says, wagging a finger in my face. "You will not wear my bra!"

I love this. She is the captain, she is a genius, but I can get under her skin this way. I suppose it's her insecurity; being a woman doesn't come naturally to her, any more than being a well-adjusted person comes to me, and I can play with that. I would never abuse it.

I kiss her forehead. She shoves me back onto the bed, and as I tumble in the rumpled sheets I catch a fleeting reflection of myself in the sliver of mirror she keeps above the dresser.

I am so young; without any gray hairs, not a speck of fat on me. Young, slim, and laughing still. She storms out in a huff, clutching a handful of fabric I imagine must be all her lingerie, leaving me amused with myself.

It takes a few minutes before I realize she has actually taken my uniform. It does make me laugh more, but I don't put on her bra. Instead I wrap myself in a sheet and dash into the corridor with my head ducked down.

K. NA

It's a joy to remember what the War was like.

There are simple things, like the alternating cold metal of outer bulkheads/hot metal of inner bulkheads that I feel as I walk back to my room, trailing one hand on the worn walls. It's just like the Bathyscaphe; details Ritry Goligh's mind replicated every time we forged to life.

I look down on a pattern hammered into the ground underfoot, several letters repeated like initials:

NA NA NA NA

Neo-Armorica, Ritry's faction in the War; a nation that barely exists anymore. Or does it exist again, because I'm here? I don't know.

There are other details I've experienced again since, like the constant musk of bodies in the air, the bland smell of tinned food after a year in storage, the alkali tang of shower water from the sub's recycling cisterns; all these things are discrete and familiar to me. They are features I could experience in any other place at any other time.

What is impossible to replicate is this overall feel of the War, hanging like a constant thickness in the air, like fluid in an artificial womb swaddling me in. It envelops me now even as I walk down the hull, perhaps some early precursor of my ability to read the bonds; a mass human redeployment that will change the face of my world forever.

I was on the frontlines in that change, and every day death was a companion. Our people were dying constantly. Our ships and mines were being lost to enemy fire even as the global tsunamis unleashed by quakeseed blasts continued to pummel our homeland; wrecking cities and destroying our bases of power.

It was apocalyptic, the real end-times, but there was a kind of transcendent joy in living on that knife-edge; in walking it with others and feeling that what we did every day could make a difference. I feel that joy again now, making every second that I'm here, wherever and whatever here is, so poignant it aches.

I have missed this.

I hurry through the subglacic, down corridors where marines I know jeer at me in a comradely way. I think I even spy Tigrates but I duck quickly out of sight. If there was anyone who would rip my towel off and laugh for months to come as I ran naked back to my quarters, it would be her.

Happily I reach my quarters without such incident and stride in, slamming the door behind me. The space is small, and Heclan is on the floor off his bed balled up in sweaty covers and groaning.

"Rit?" he mumbles, still drunk from the CSF bender we went on last night. "Turn off the light."

"It is off, you idiot," I slur back at him. I'm still drunk too, I suppose. Most of the crew is, most of the time.

I turn the light on and the room flickers to yellow life.

"Stop it, I'm dying," Heclan moans.

He's short, quite ugly and a crazy little bastard. Already half-bald, with scrags of wispy brown hair standing up on the side of his head like static from where he's been curled up like an unwanted dog, I wouldn't want anyone else for my jack assistant. Being ugly has never stopped him making off with a wide range of women, some even combat marines, using his inestimable persistence. The man never stops, has some unknowable well of confidence and competence I've never scraped the surface of, and that gives him a charm many can't resist. It's what kept me from killing him when he injected alcohol directly into my brain instead of CSF coolant.

He flaps a hand vaguely upward. "Light, dying."

"Hurry up and die then," I tell him, acting out the script just as I remember it without even needing to think, "or get up, we have to go inject some engrams for this latest raid."

"I'll take you with me when I die," he mumbles, shielding his eyes. "At least shade the light."

I look up at the light, recessed into the ceiling to avoid potential injury, like everything on the sub. There's a folded bit of burnt yellow fabric held over it with magnetic clamps, a shade jury-rigged to reduces the glare. I remember this detail now; how we went through a few of these towels a month as the light burnt them out. This latest one is almost burnt through.

I pull the shade down and Heclan sighs contentedly. By the yellowish light I look around the room, my room, where I spent so many years of my life. It is a tight galley spread liberally with empty CSF jars smuggled out of the lab, with two narrow cots piled with rumpled clothing, a slim ravine between them filled with Heclan and sheets, and shelves which have mostly been stacked with mismatched Soul Jacker journals scavenged from various raids, all in different languages. Every inch of the panel floor is covered in clothes, dirty plates, and other garbage: assorted note-papers covered in my scrawly ink, several of Heclan's collection of pottery owls, shoes, ski-poles which Heclan and I used to use for 'deck-hiking' around the sub on our shifts off; all of it scattered from various cubbyhole shelves and inbuilt cupboards.

The room looks like a dry-ice bomb hit it.

"What happened here?" I ask Heclan.

He rolls to look up at me, squinting against the light. "Mouse," he mumbles weakly.

Ah, yes, I remember. We had gotten extremely drunk after fixing that blinded marine, then we'd started searching for a mouse sometime in the middle of the night, because of a sound one of us thought we'd heard. At some point I went to find Ven to ask her help in hunting it.

"Did she wear warpaint?" Heclan asks.

I laugh, remembering that part of our conversation too. So that's where the image came from.

"No paint. Now get up." I prod him firmly with my toe. He groans more loudly the more I toe him, which is exactly as it should be. I play a tune off his skin, and he groans differently when I poke his belly and when I poke his face, until finally he starts to rouse.

I sit on the cot, dizzy myself, while he stumbles to his feet. I'm still drunk, of course. My head feels too heavy, and once more I try to make sense of where and what I am. I still feel like Me, one seventh of Ritry Goligh, but I remember being Ritry Goligh too. I remember Solfeje, and my heart beats a little harder at that.

Is she here? Is she waiting? Is this the race we've both stumbled into?

"I'm up!" Heclan declares abruptly and proudly, as if I've been badgering him all this time.

"About time," I say, and give him a boot in the butt. He lurches against the wall with his pants around his knees, banging his head hard. We both laugh even as a trickle of blood runs down from a split in his temple.

"Am I cut?" he asks between gasps of laughter, holding out his fingers with red on them. "Is this blood?"

I was such a jerk. We both were, and the constant threat of impending death made it all seem like good fun. Getting wasted and smacking our bodies around was really just our way of taking what little we had control and using it to spit in death's face.

"You'll be fine, just walk it off."

We get dressed. We scrub our faces to get rid of the blear and the worst of the alcohol stink. I help Heclan put on a small plastic bandage, then we head out for the jack-bay.

L. MINDBOMB

There is an unspoken hierarchy on a subglacic.

I recall this as we walk along the narrow corridors together. Top of the heap were the combat marines, without question. I was one of them at the start of my military draft, before my aptitude in an EMR highlighted me for special training.

The combat marines fought together, died together and came back with booty together. We were the jocks in our training camps, the coolest kids who got all the best sex, cherry-picking whomever we wanted from the lower rungs on the ladder. We made our own tribe to which few others were admitted, because who could understand the sheer madness of what we faced when shunted out the conning tower assault tubes?

Next came command. Ven was in this group, at its head. Even she would demur to the combat marines at times, for morale. She ordered these men and women to their deaths; that could only work if she showed them the respect that risk demanded.

Beneath command lay all the numerous administration fields, the marines who didn't fight, from those who worked the radar room (low) to those who stocked the small-arms vault (medium) and manned the subglacic's weapons array (high). Beneath them was logistics, the subclass who didn't come close to the fighting and supported those who did, including cooking, cleaning and managing stock in the commissary.

At the edge of them all, isolated from any kind of standard hierarchy by the confessional nature of the job, were me and Heclan, the Soul Jackers. While essential to the success of any mission, integral to it in ways even the captain didn't always fully understand, it could be hard sometimes to argue we were necessary. Everything the ship had to do, it could do without us. You could not say that about anyone else on board. Even the guy who cleaned the nozzles in the chicken soup machine was more vital than me.

Yet a good Soul Jacker could change the entire crew. I'd seen it on other ships and learned it as a combat marine before they ever redeployed me. The best Soul Jackers provided a dozen essential support roles all rolled into one powerful package: absolver to marines who couldn't deal with the constant loss of comrades and needed select memories expunged forever; priest to people who believed in no god but still needed to feel a higher power watching over them; physical consort to the lost, the lonely, the frightened; psychologist to men and women who trusted no one and had felt their own minds blown inward by combat; most-trusted teacher of all kinds of EMR-injectable skills.

We had detailed files on every member of the crew, and I knew that kind of power and access could lead to mistrust and doubt as often as it did to higher morale. I'd heard of cases of abuse where Soul Jackers used their position to rape their way through a crew, Lagging the memories after they'd had their fill. I'd heard of spies posing as Soul Jackers, come from other factions in the War to drain all a crew's secrets and weaknesses without anyone even knowing it had happened, leading to an intrinsic mistrust. I'd also heard of incompetency, in cases where Jackers could not stomach the things they had to do, or were unable to do them in the face of intense battle pressure. Most of all, I heard of burnouts.

They happened all the time. War-Jackers had to weigh the mental wellbeing of everyone on board; we were known for our ability to 'feel' the emotional state of the ship. Now I know this 'feeling' as the bonds, but back then it was a vague idea even the best researchers were unable to pin down despite generations of jacking into the mind. We sensed it though there was no good name for it, and we were the ones best placed to apply a nudge here and a prod there to turn the mood around, for just as long as we could hold ourselves together.

We fixed problems. We hacked into living minds and made them right again, ready to serve again as fodder for the War, like the man with the lost eyes. If I hadn't 'fixed' him he would eventually have pulled his whole combat brigade down and gotten other marines killed.

Instead I erased his weaknesses. Now he'll alienate his old friends but he'll find new ones that match the man he's become. He was a broken cog and I hammered him true, but it wasn't all I did back then. The best Soul Jackers wielded their power in every social instance, and I was the best.

I had the crew's implicit trust. Having fought in combat myself, I'd been through all the worst things there were. Hardened killers came to me to weep and bitch and moan without any sense of shame, and often I could solve their problems without ever needing an invasive jack; just a word in the right ear, a quick roll in my regulation single bed, or a debauched evening slugging back strong CSF vodka.

That was the true role of a Soul Jacker; the beating heart of a ship. So Tigrates and Ferrily partied with us, drawn to our invisible mystique. So Ven fell in love with me despite herself, entranced by the compassionate depths of her own Soul that being near me exposed. So I drank to keep myself in balance as the world spun wildly on, and we all played our roles and we all stayed alive through the long grim haul of the War.

"Ritry," Heclan says abruptly, yanking me from the reverie. He's standing by the door to the jack-bay while I've walked clear past it. I toss a goofy grin and turn around.

There are already three marines waiting outside, ready to be fixed. I nod at them and enter the room. It is barely bigger than our quarters, half-filled with the gray metal donut of the EMR machine with Heclan's control screen beside it. The walls are lined with locked cupboards that stretch back into the hull, filled with all the supplies we need.

I pick up a tablet and scan through the manifest. Ten marines are on our docket for the morning, all of them needing engrams of the best schematics we have of an Aleutian hydrate mine and its defenses, spotted on a spy satellite pass.

It'll be a long but simple day, as the knowledge is light and the routes to embed it well-trodden. I groan at Heclan and he pulls a face back at me. I can't describe how good it feels to be here again, contributing as part of this team, even if I don't know what I'm supposed to be doing. I'm glad to play along.

"Send them in," I tell Heclan.

He clicks a button to open the door and shouts through it. "Next!"

A marine comes in. He's massive, square, but vulnerable in this place. There's something familiar about his eyes but I put that to one side as I wink cheerily, putting him at ease. Every crew-member knows their relationship with me is not a normal one. He says something insulting about me screwing the commander in my towel, which suggests Tigrates did see me in flight earlier. I reply with something bright about him maybe coming away from this jack with an inexplicable desire to screw his own asshole. He chuckles and winces. This is my rapport.

The familiarity grows stronger as Heclan straps him in for the jack, and I try to puzzle it out. Perhaps we drank together once? Fought together on an old hydrate raid? It's only when he is slid into the EMR like a half-rack of ribs, and I'm lying by his side scanning through the outer layers of his Molten Core that I remember how I know him.

I've lost most of it now, bait I used a long time ago to keep myself alive, but I'll never forget the basic texture of this man's Soul. I lived off it for hours, spooning chunks at a time to the Lag while I was trapped inside his mind. I cannibalized him to save myself.

Oh fuck. Realization hits me like a tsunami.

Today is the day we get mindbombed.

I pull out of his outer thoughts sharply, snatch up the tablet and stare at the time display for long seconds as the weight of this sinks in.

The mindbomb is coming. In less than an hour everybody aboard this ship will be dead.

ME

17. ART

We descend like liquid into porous rock.

Two of my hands find passageways in the back of the monk's cloister cells, one finds a hole in the kitchen beneath a rusted metal oven, two rappel down to the anchorite hutches carved in the cliff and discover a rabbits warren of narrow tunnels.

At their head I run deep into a labyrinth of pitch-black caverns filled with memories of horror; past a hewn-rock crèche where the infant brood made finger paintings with blood, past a hall where children extracted the living organs of victims and strung them still pumping around the walls, past the cracked canvases of their latter artworks; exploded diagrams of the human nervous system made of slit-out nerve networks splayed like fractal tree branches, judged by the quality of screams they drew. Further in I pass hulking EMRs and medical equipment, everything the teenaged brood needed to section living Souls, and the precursor of the tortures King Ruin perpetrated on me in his experimental Court.

It's horrific, but I don't give a shit about any of it. I've seen and lived this for years now, and none of it is not what the immured Soul fears most. He was an earnest part of all these exercises in pain; he wound out the guts, he splayed the nerves, he flattened the minds with just as much gusto as the rest of the brood. Rather he is afraid of something far more terrible.

Then I'm there.

The tunnel ends at a rough octagonal chamber in the rock, with seven tall redbrick walls facing me at faceted angles, weirdly bright in the suit lights. The air smells stale and ancient but for an acrid tang of human effluent, reminding me of the mud-filled central sepulcher in the middle of Mr. Ruin's ancient pyramid of memory.

A shrine to past sicknesses.

In the center of the octagon lies a large stack of red clay bricks set upon a wooden pallet. Beside them sits a squat gray portable generator, its cables lost in dust, and a blue barrel with a TOXIC label on its side.

I stride closer and detect the smell of burnt hydrates on the air. I circle the brick stack and see a motorized cement mixer lying on its side, the same kind Skulk-crews in proto-Calico use to mortar their jetsam buildings together.

I kneel beside it, resting my fingers lightly on the equipment's rough lip. There are many bonds here at this deepest point; a thousand sedimentary layers of suffering. Here victims were sacrificed, here brood members were punished, here King Ruin held frequent cannibalistic survival games amongst those coming of age to cull out the weak. The strongest bond by far though is the terror. There is one Soul here, now, and it has long gone mad with fear.

I walk to the reddest, most freshly bricked wall from which the terror emanates like a cold Arctic wind. A brick wall fits crudely within a carved rock archway, perhaps leading to deeper tunnels. I touch the rough fired clay and the terror beyond hits me like an electrostatic shock, focused and desperate. I slide my hand into the slim gap at the edge, and feel the madness of his Sunken World.

One of my hands passes me a pickaxe, and the terror beyond redoubles.

"I'm coming," I say, and swing the pick hard into the brick.

18. SUNKEN WORLD

The wall is fifteen layers thick of brick and takes hours to smash through, swapping in and out for my hands. The terror beyond heightens until at last, as I break through the final brick screen into darkness, the heart of this desperate creature overloads in a flurry of staccato beats.

I punch through the gap into the foul stench of bodily waste, and drop to my knees by a translucent-white cave thing, lank and slack and naked in its own filth, lying on the shit-strewn floor and palsying in death.

Down one side of the wide tunnel are more brick-stacks, with another cement mixer, fuel supply, generator, cables and buckets. Down the other side are numerous pallets stacked tall with cans of food. Down the middle is an open sewer of waste. In the cave thing's hand there's a mortaring trowel, with a bucket of shiny wet cement and a small heap of bright red bricks nearby.

It has been immuring itself.

A hand passes me a syringe concocted from the tanker's Soul Jacker lab. I stab it into this creature's heart and depress the plunger. Epinephrine jolts him back to life, and he opens his wide eyes on me and starts to scream.

I punch him silent in the bonds then jack through his mind's weak crystalline shell and deep into the tsunami-blasted mire of his rotten Sunken World.

The mountains of shit inside are epic.

I stand atop my Bathyscaphe alone after passing through slurry, looking out over a rotting landscape. The stench is overpowering; I can smell it even through my sublavic suit's HUD, seeping into everything. All around lie the remnants of a Molten Core torn to shreds. There are scraps of buildings and pyramids, features that were once whole memories but have since been gnawed at and partially consumed.

The black mud of mulched memory is everywhere. I look up to a lowering dark sky. I look to the horizon to see a low tsunami rolling in, the hint of Lag worms leaping like froth on its crest. In the other direction I see a shoddy White Tower.

Fuck this.

I don't have time for it. I've been this way before and I know what caused it: an overpowering engram inject of nonsense knowledge, too much for the brain to handle. I did it to Mr. Ruin, and from everything I'm sensing this mind did it to itself.

I turn to the Bathyscaphe, flick a switch in my mind and it becomes a Dactyl helicopter. I swing into the cab and fire up the dual-rotors, pull back on the stick and this machine that is me jerks upward with a roar. I give it the commands and it soars toward the White Tower.

Bofors rockets take out the soldiers on the wall, dressed in a medley of ancient armor, all leather and chained mail. My howitzers rake the Tower's doorway, blowing it inward enough for me to see the piles of heaped garbage inside, some bastard's mementoes I don't care about.

I thrust the stick back and take us lurching up into the sky, toward the peak where the Tower is still whitest and gleaming, where a door to the aetheric bridge should stand. In seconds I reach the peak and blow it to dust in a hailstorm of rockets and shells.

I grapnel into the gap and tie off the elasteel line to my Dactyl, left hovering in place behind me like a moored boat. The aetheric bridge stands behind a colonnaded door to my right, and right in front of me, cowering against a clamshell-wall now striated with ash and burn-marks, huddles the same figure I found in the immured cave.

He's gibbering, but I don't expect him to talk. Rather I stride in, crack his head open and look at what's left inside. Snatches of memory come bubbling up through the mud of his mind and I see myself:

- loading a Soul Jacker's syringe with silver liquid, my hands trembling. I am surrounded in the bonds by dozens of others now, my brood class all gathered together in a grand suicidal pact. As one we lift the glinting steel to our eyes, push the needles in and depress the plungers.

The rush that follows is awful, destructive, terrifying, but it can't

Soul Killer

wipe it all. Nothing can wipe away the fear.

Another memory bubbles up, of sitting in the classroom in the circular turret when I was just a brood child. With the others I am flicking pins into the open stomach cavity of a screaming woman, when one of our cadaver lecturers enters with a new boy in tow.

He is flaxen-haired, gaunt and covered in blood. His mouth is mired with it, his eyes are wild with it, his teeth are stained with it.

The pin-flicking stops. All eyes turn to look at him; a new brood member older than most when they're brought in. All of us can feel the hate burning up off him, with none of the fear new inductees usually show when they arrive.

His hate is overwhelming. He hates the hand at his back, hates the Suns themselves, hates himself and the things he has done. It sends a chill in my blood. He looks at us like we are nothing, the same way we look at the victims the Suns brings for us to play with.

I know at once that he is now the predator and we are the prey.

One of the girls doesn't realize this quickly enough, and flicks a pin at him. It bounces off his cheek, and he reaches out through the bonds in a way I've never seen before. At once the girl begins to choke. She grabs for her throat, rises to her feet, then a fountain of blood and entrails spews up from her mouth.

She dies while we watch. None of us has ever seen this before. The Suns hasn't taught it to us.

The cadaver teacher grins. "This is a new boy in the school," it says. "One day he'll be your general. Play nice."

I look at the boy and he looks at me, one amongst many. In his eyes I see not only death, but emptiness forever, and it turns my bowels to water.

The boy walks in and takes a seat. The memory fades.

Another rises up.

I have made my own successes, brought my own minor atrocities down upon the small circle of the world to which I have been assigned, these islands off Ankara, and the Suns has begun to notice me. I am not yet invited to the deeper research Courts, I have never joined an experimental jack into the Solid Core, but perhaps one day

I will. I am a sergeant on the frontlines in the Suns' ceaseless war against the world, and that is fair, that is right, I am no general of the brood yet.

Then one man changes everything. Ritry Goligh. I feel it as he breaks open the aetheric bridge for the first time since the Suns first did it millennia ago; the shockwave reverberates across the world. The ground I have been raised to stand upon all my life shifts, and I no longer know the things I thought I knew.

Moments later the call comes out from the Suns to soothe us: the event is localized, the matter contained, it is nothing to be concerned about. Moments after comes its warning echo from the boy covered in blood, a general now in the experimental Courts, jacking deeper than any have before. In his warning I feel his old hate swelling up again, and the sense of promise this new development offers him.

The bridge has yielded, and will yield again. In the ruins of the aether a new King will stand, and at that King's hands the void will come for us all.

Another memory rises.

It is months after Ritry Goligh killed the Suns, and I am underground in a bunker Court, afraid every day. I feel it as the first of my brood-class disappears. We all feel it, our peer-group from the monastery, bound tightly through the bonds of childhood no matter where we are in the world.

The bloody boy is coming for us, and will kill us all.

But this is worse than death. I feel it on the bonds as my old brood-mate is destroyed in an erasure more complete than the Lag, so total it rubs him out completely, unwriting a past that now never happened, a role that one of us played that is now being un-played.

I try to cling to the frame of his memory as it dissipates from my mind, but it is wrenched away just as viciously as he killed that first girl, not just in the bonds or in my mind but from the aether too. My old brood-mate never now lived. He has been wholly undone and unwritten.

Who? I can't remember. There is just the gouge where something important had been.

Days later another disappears. This time I feel the bonds distend, opening outward into a void far from the cocooning light cast by the Suns, far from the light of all Souls and into the empty blackness at the fringes of the aether.

There I feel screaming. I glimpse a loss of self that is all-pervading. I hear a Soul blown a million miles wide with nothing inside, lost but cursed with consciousness. Into that nothing-space another one of my peers is pushed.

Then she too is gone. I remember only the faintest echo of what once might have been.

More follow. Those of us who knew the bloody boy in the monastery disappear one by one. Our trails are expunged, our contributions removed, every trace we left smoothed away.

We come together. We fall apart. We gather syringes in a bid to keep our immortal Souls within the sphere of the aether. This is the path the boy has prepared for us and herded us toward. We sob into each other's minds, groping to describe a terror not even the Suns knew how to teach.

The Suns' rule is plainly over. It is the dawn of a new age now, and in it we can only hope to hide. So we load the syringes and inject ourselves. Our brains flood with noise to disguise who we really are, and give us a place to hide.

Afterward there is chaos like an ocean in a vacuum, a billion droplets scouring and rushing in tsunamis of nonsense. My mind foams into gas and back to liquid, clashing and tossing and reforming, neutering myself at an unspoken command.

But is it enough, a voice asks me, as I chew the heads off toads and bite down on barnacle shells to survive. Is it enough?

I find the bricks, mortar and materials where I left them, buried in the depths of a bond mountain so dense even he won't see the dregs of me beneath it all. I brick myself in layer after layer, until I can't hear anything from the world, and surely he can't hear me.

Still I plead to god, whatever that creature is, to not abandon me. I want to exist. I want to have existed. I want to rejoin the aether when I die.

Please don't let him steal my immortal Soul.

I pull out with screams ringing in my ears. I'm in the cave and the terror has infected me too.

I too have looked into this bloody boy's eyes and seen the hate; I have seen him as the brood-King sweeping down across the aether to erase everyone I love, and I recognize the hatred that fuels him on. In this alone, I know him. It springs from the same empty rage that I felt all my life until I found my place in the War, that returned as a numb sense of unbelonging after the fighting was over, when I lived on a Skulk just waiting for the next tsunami to come and rub me away.

I have known this feeling all my life; that nothing I do means a thing, that my suffering and my happiness both are nothing and so the suffering and happiness of are nothing too.

The feeling encircles me in old madness, and I fear a return to this more than anything else. I have lost everyone already, all my friends, lovers, and family that gave my life meaning; all I have left is my own Soul.

But the stakes are too high to protect it any longer. I would rather lose myself forever than let the brood-King keep what he has taken; not Ray, Doe, Far, So, La or Ti, not Loralena or Art or Mem, not Carrolla or Don Zachary or Ven or Heclan or Ferrily or Tigrates or even Mr. Ruin. This is our world and our lives all mattered, and I cannot allow them to be eradicated so.

All life has meaning. All life is worth something, and this is where I draw the line, like a little voice speaking in my mind saying 'wrong, wrong, wrong.' Life matters, and there is nothing I will not do to fight for it.

I ascend from the caves and into the light, my hands carrying the cave creature behind us. I stand in the cloisters breathing the fresh salt air, looking out over the ocean and the tanker, out over the bonds in this cliff-top monastery stretching back millennia, out to the limits of my HUD's EMR Wall, and know what I am going to do.

Adapt, learn and conquer.

--.

M. TRAP

Holding the tablet in my hand in the jack-bay, looking at the digital clock tick down to the mindbomb that will kill the crew, the possibilities race through my head. Maybe this is why I am here. I could save them. I could change everything.

If this is even real. I don't know what it means. Am I hunting Solfeje or am I really back here and this is it, and right now the seconds are ticking down to the moment Ven and all my friends die?

The slate wipes clean on that last thought. It feels like I'm here, and if there's even the smallest chance that's true I have to do something right now.

I drop the tablet, kick out of the EMR tray and bolt out of the jack-bay door, ignoring Heclan as he calls after me.

"Ritry, what the hell are you doing?"

I'm doing something I've dreamed of for the last twenty-three years.

The corridors of this old subglacic blur around me like memory fading to magma, a passage I never took because I never knew what was coming. Exhilaration fills me up because I'm finally changing things, finally saving them all. I race up through the decks planning what I'll say and how I'll make the threat real.

I burst into the dizzy heights of the conning tower with T-minus fifty minutes to spare. The tower is what it always was; screens and readouts and an atmosphere of humming. tension. Crew-members stand at blinking stations circled around the metal walls with Ven in the middle at the periscope, her pale face now looking back at me with a quizzical expression.

I approach her and speak in the hushed tones the conning tower requires.

"Captain, may I speak with you please?"

"Not now, Mr. Goligh," she says. "I'm currently engaged."

I don't say, "I know," as that would be foolish in the extreme. I don't blurt out the threat we're facing, because in full view of all these others I'd have to explain how I know it, when the only good explanation is that I'm either incompetent or a spy.

"Please," I say instead, "it's important."

She looks at me. She looks to her lietenant and gives a sharp nod. "Two minutes. Follow me."

She strides down the narrow corridor to the captain's hutch and I follow, down past racks of weaponry and emergency exposure suits. In the small space that is her ready room she leans against her desk and crosses her arms. I'm briefly surprised that the walls and ceiling are not filled with little numbered lockers, but of course that was never a real thing.

"What is it, Ritry?" Ven asks.

I appreciate this, that she respects me enough to bring me back here. She knows I'm not a fool even though I act like it at times.

"I've got reason to believe this ship is about to be mindbombed," I say quietly. "In less than fifty minutes. We're moving into an ambush and everybody on board will die if you don't do something about it."

Ven's face changes, her curiosity becoming concern. "An ambush? What reason do you have to believe this?"

I press on, because if I have to rely on the reason I have to believe this, I've already lost her. "There's a proto-Rusk hydrate mine ahead of us that was hit hard by the Aleut, is that right?" I don't wait for confirmation; there's no way I should know even this much. "They've got several ships filled with the wounded and you're thinking about offering them an escort." Her eyes narrow and I plow on, the words spilling out in a flurry; information I gathered long after the mindbomb dropped and they were all dead. "I know our treaty with the proto-Rusk requires us to assist them, but we can't do it this time. The raid's just a cover to steal this ship and its information; the first blow in a counter-strike that'll see neo-Armorica driven out of the Arctic for good. I promise you, Ven, we need to bomb those ships or we need to turn around and run right now."

Ven's concern hardens to displeasure. "I'll ask you again, Ritry, how do you know any of this?"

"Scan the ships," I answer, because I've got no source she'll believe; not that I already lived through all this once and have regretted that survival every day since. "Scan them and you'll see there's an army out there, lowboats and dropships ready to ensnare us. The motherlode of intelligence they get from us will be enough to put us permanently behind in the War. Plus we'll all be dead. At least scan them, Ven, you'll see I'm right."

At that moment firm hands take hold of my arms from behind, locking me in place. I turn my head and see two burly security marines at my back. I didn't even hear them coming in. I was too preoccupied to notice Ven summon them through the panic button under her desk.

"Let this all be a mistake, Mr. Goligh," Ven says, a hint of agony creeping through her mounting anger. "Just another bad joke, or tell me now how you know this."

I open my mouth and put desperate words into it, a story that paints me as incompetent but at least not a spy.

"From a jack," I say. "I read it in the last round of captives."

Ven's cold anger wrinkles. "Captives? The last round was three weeks ago. Have you held onto this information for three weeks and told no one?"

I begin to feel her slipping away from me. She's disengaging more as a person every second and I need to do something. I glance up at the display behind her desk; forty-five minutes remain. From what I remember the trap was a pincer movement of proto-Rusk and Aleut nation ships, encircling us long before the mindbomb fell. They had every eventuality covered.

"I just put the pieces together now," I say. "If nothing else, do a radar scan of the icebergs and the mine, you'll see they're loaded with unexpected density. Those will be Dactyls and subglacics, shielded by the ice."

"Or medical supplies," Ven answers, the anger briefly surfacing. "Do you realize this is a drop we've had scheduled for months? I don't know who told you it was an Aleut raid, or an escort. We're here to pick up medicines for the entire neo-Armorican fleet, a mission classified to tower-crew only."

This completely throws me.

"What?" I blurt. It makes no sense, and doesn't sync with what I learned in the aftermath. There's no resupply scheduled for months. I shake my head. "That's not right. It's a proto-Rusk question of passage, it's a trap, that's what I know."

"What you know," Ven says slowly, like she's tasting the words. Then she draws the pistol at her waist and points it at my face. My eyes go wide. This is not how I envisaged this going. "What else do you know, Mr. Goligh?"

"Ven, it's me."

"No, it isn't. You're lying, Ritry. You're talking about things you shouldn't know and asking me to bomb a supply drop the War-effort badly needs. Why?"

"What? No, I'm trying to save us, trying to save you."

"What was the marine's name?" she asks, holding the pistol steady in my face. "The one you jacked three weeks ago who gave you this information, which you've only figured out now. Tell me her name."

I have no idea. I gave all this away a long time ago to the Lag. I could guess, but how many names are there in the world?

"I didn't memorize it. I didn't think anything of it at the time."

"So tell me what she looked like. Tell me what her ship was called. Tell me anything to corroborate your story."

I can't.

"Scan the ships," I say, pleading now. "Scan the hydrate mine. You'll see I'm right."

"I'll do nothing. Running those scans could be a signal. Doing anything you say could be a signal. What is your intent here, Soul Jacker?"

The address by my profession comes like a blow, like an insult. She's making the distance she needs to blow my brains out here and now, in the hutch, for gross espionage.

"I'm trying to save us."

"With three-week-old information you never mentioned, from a marine whose name you don't know, at a vital supply drop for the fleet? Either you're more incompetent than I ever dreamed possible, or you're a spy and this is an attempt to spoil a top-secret pickup."

She said it. Spy.

I was wrong, and I realize now how wrong I've been all along, all my life since she died. I always thought it was the compassion I brought out in her that caused her to fall for the ambush, but she was never that unprofessional. She put that face on for me but as captain she was hard all the way through. It wasn't compassion that led her to 'help' the proto-Rusk, but a secret neo-Armorican supply run that met with a proto-Rusk betrayal that none of us saw coming.

I was wrong about so much. My mind races with the story I could have told, something she might have believed, but what? I can think of nothing that would have helped. I can't tell her I've come from a Hollow Star in the depths of the aether, that I'm hunting a half-pulse marine named Solfeje in search of, what? I can't tell her that in my world she is dead and has been dead since this moment, which I've regretted ever since.

Twenty-three years of regret. No matter what I can't let that happen again.

I close my eyes and focus. This mind doesn't have the pathways; hasn't had them forced open by Mr. Ruin, by the godships, by overload, but I remember how and that'll have to do. Standing there with Ven's pistol to my head, I jack into the bonds.

Rushing through electrostatic then magma, I reach into Ven's mind and Lag away all her doubts. I draw on the unified strength of the crew below and reach wider, for seconds making all these people my hands.

Ritry Goligh's young mind creaks under the unaccustomed torrent I'm forcing through it, but there is time to feel that pain later. For now I make the security officers holding me let go and back away. I have an operator in the conning tower run the radar scans I need, and find the dense blocks I'm looking for; small stealth ships encircling us front and back, hiding behind the hydrate mine and icebergs.

They have corralled us already, and there is no going back.

I relinquish control of the crew, holding only onto Ven. I have her click another button on her desk to open a comm line with the tower, and through her throat I give the order.

"Ready every marine troop and lowboat," she says. "Ready every dry-ice bomb and missile in the arsenal. Send a coded message for support to the fleet asking for immediate, mass reinforcements. In thirty minutes we raise the EMR shield and attack that mine."

There's outrage, shock, defiance in her eyes as she realizes what I'm doing. I hate to see it but I hold her there still.

"Do it," I make her bark, "now!"

Reaching back into the conning tower, I give the first of her lieutenants a quick massage, enough to get her moving and sending orders out into the ship-wide system, which is enough to get the others moving too.

I'm suddenly exhausted.

I have Ven sit behind her desk and I slump across from her, feeling the urgency pass into the crew. Alerts sound. Feet stamp metal floors as they rush to War-stations. Before me Ven struggles against my stranglehold on her intent, and I know she will never forgive me for this.

"I'm sorry," I say. "I promise, I'm trying to keep you alive."

We sit and stare at each other. I feel the ties of love between us break and I weather it. To keep her alive, surely this is worth it. Why else have I been sent back?

"I'll go with them," I say, hoping to explain. "I'll fight too. You'll see."

She sits and judges me. She judges herself, feeling a fool for ever trusting me. She let me into her mind and into her bed, and now she's retreating further behind the layer of ice she's kept for so long. Now she hates me and she'll never trust another person this much again.

Nothing will be the same.

N. CHORD

Thirty minutes pass and by the end I'm panting, drained from holding her in place. Any uncertainty she might have felt is long gone, replaced by ice-cold conviction. Now she is planning how she will kill me, when she gets the chance.

She won't get it. The subglacic beneath us hums with the sound of marines stamping into their assault lowboats and readying weapons, with the clank and shuffle of missiles being loaded into bays.

This is the flagship of the neo-Armorican fleet; best-armed, best-equipped, best-prepared. Reinforcements will come soon to keep us safe. History will change.

I rise to my feet.

"Manage the battle," I tell Ven. She stares up at me, whiter than I ever remember. "You'll see soon enough that I've saved us. If you still want to kill me after that, if any of us survive, I won't fight it. I love you, I've always loved you, and I'm sorry I didn't do this better."

I stride out. I keep a loose rein on her even as I smooth my passage through the ship, descending ladderways to a lowboat assault bay where combat marines are standing ready, where I always truly belonged. I should never have let them make me a Soul Jacker. I push amongst them until Ferrily is at my side, in full battle gear and frowning.

"The fuck you doing here, Rit?"

I pull down a white subglacic HUD and combat armor from the wall-rack nearby and start bolting it on. "Leading you," I say.

She laughs. I flip the switch in her mind so that she believes it.

"Well all right then," she says, and hollers for the marines to hear, fifteen in this bay, the complement for one lowboat, and they shut up.

"Soul Jacker's leading the run," she shouts. "All clear?"

"All clear," they shout back.

They know me. They trust Ferrily. We're going to fight together.

I love it.

This was always my true addiction. Not jacking in like Far, not alcohol like Ritry, not even dying, but this. I am addicted to leading a chord into battle, ever-ready to die for the people I love.

What I love is Ven, and that dizzy bastard Heclan, and the marines by my side and everyone in this ship. I'm ready to die for them all, and they are ready to die for me. We're in this together.

It's the best drug I've ever felt.

I get into my hatch in the lowboat as the door raises and latch myself in to the protective webbing across the narrow bench-seat. All across the subglacic's belly this will be happening, in twenty different lowboats set to jet up through the water and emerge behind the stealth boats waiting for us.

I cycle my HUD up. It'll be no protection against a mindbomb, we hadn't invented shields that small yet, and the readout is more simplistic than anything I had when I jacked the Molten Core, but I can hear the breathing and the voices of my fellow marines spread out in a supersized chord around me. I can see simple information about their positions relative to me displayed in the faceplate.

Fifteen is twice seven plus one, I think idly, as a computer voice counts down from T-minus ten minutes until launch. Two chords of seven like two almighty fists of god, falling to crush their enemies, with me fighting right in their midst.

I see that I loved these days and the War so well because I was never alone. I belonged so intensely, I had a family that I'd kill and die for, and when the mindbomb fell I lost it all. I've missed these days ever since, because emptiness was all that followed.

T-minus one, and the lowboat is driven sideways out of the subglacic with a propulsive thump that rocks us all in our seats, then the jet-screw fires and hammers us back into our webbing, rocketing up through the ice-fogged Arctic water like a missile hoving in for an explosion.

I relinquish Ven, the bonds of control stretched taut by distance. An instant later the EMR shield goes up around the subglacic, she's safe, and then we burst through the water and the battle begins.

O. COUNTER-RAID

The benches deploy like rail-guns into the gray spray of the Arctic, spitting us out on a flat and rocking platform while the lowboat's munition-racks peel open and shoot up, thrusting a fully-loaded howitzer chaingun through the llowboat's hull and into my hands.

I fire.

All around us are the vaulting canyons of glaciers, like dirty white cliffs in a labyrinth, thrashed by foaming gray waves. There is the stink of refined hydrates on the air and the buffeting of a freezing wind that reaches even through my subglacic suit to chill my blood, matched to the rattle and thump of the cannon in my hands.

I know this world. I fought in it countless times then lived through it countless times more in the minds of broken marines. I led the first mission of my chord into the heart of the Solid Core, and I can do this shit in my sleep.

Chaingun fire erupts around me and my own rounds strafe foam out of the ocean, homing in on the low hump of a stealthship surfacing through the water ahead. It is a low, poorly-armored oblong designed to evade sonar more than for combat. It turns rapidly, trying to deploy its meager guns and spit out its complement of marines.

We give it no such chance; our hail of depleted plutonium shells bites into it, striking sparks and chewing through its thin bulkheads into the crawlspaces within. It unleashes only one rocket before it explodes in a fireball of metal and surf, caught from beneath by a Bofors torpedo.

"Off-boat!" I shout through the HUD, then dive from the lowboat platform into the water. Five seconds later it explodes spectacularly as the stealth ship's missile finds it.

Dim cheering comes through the HUD from my fellow marines, followed quickly by Ferrily on a private channel.

"Fucking lead then, Rit."

The freezing water sucks at my suit but the air caps in its joints keep me easily afloat, and I circle propelled by the mini-screw in the small of my back. I can't see anything but chasms and caverns of dirty bluish ice, but in the HUD map I see the blips of our lowboats taking on other ships in the ambush arc. I look up to the mining rig, far above through hundreds of tons of solid ice.

That'll be where the mindbomb is, and where the munitions are thickest. The HUD displays the rig's wire-frame schematics atop the ice, pulsing red where the deep drill bit is coring the ice-bed, releasing the hydrates that have fuelled this War and will transform the shape of our world in years to come.

"Up the cliff," I call through the HUD, over the rushing sound of ice cracking and breakers striking the hissing ruin of the stealthship. I mark the ice-face purple on their screens. "Two squads of seven left and right, low-slalom to encircle and infiltrate, I'll run central pivot, go."

"Don't need to tell me twice," Ferrily calls back, and already I see she is firing her ice-hook upward, catching in the pack and reeling herself up. She bobs twice off the water, skating like a pro along the surface as the slack on the line gets taken in then she's ascending and the rest follow; fourteen of them flowing like white fire up the ice.

I take center point.

Thirty seconds later we breast the glacier top, and the wind howls hard enough to blow us off our feet. The storm is blinding here, snow whipping harshly across my HUD.

"Down!" I shout and we lay flat with practiced movements on the ice, getting into a linked-up slalom-chain with feet locked to shoulders.

"Fire."

The marine at the tail fires the jet-propellant pack and we shoot off over the ice. Ferrily steers this human train from the front, sliding us over the wind-scoured upper surface in a human train, circling chasms and ice spikes, while the rest of us lie still with our Kaos rifles out. She's aiming for the great iron bulk of the mine, squatting over the ice like a beast feeding on a carcass.

I crane my head back and howl into the HUD, riding the thrill of imminent engagement. I'm turning everything around now and I'm doing it myself, not hidden away in the relative safety of the Soul jack-bay. I was always meant to be a combat marine out here with my chord. Answering howls rise up from in front and in back; the high of the pack.

We rush in and glimpse flashes of the mine through thick flurries of snow caught in cross-glacier gales. It looks like the one at Spartan's Crag but bigger, set atop five metal boles sunk deep into the ice and heaped up with a confusion of rusted gantries, walkways, lookouts, rigging and weaponry nests, painted with a thick veneer of crusted snow. At the top a hot plume of steam pulses out in hacking coughs, spewing invisible pollutants from the refining process along with frequent methane burps of fire.

Figures are moving up there now, running into position and taking up weapons. They must be stunned at our sudden assault. This was to be their great coup, taking a neo-Armorican flagship without a single shot fired, an historical rout. Now it's suddenly a hot war they weren't prepared for.

Ferrily swerves us and we snake jerkily to the left; seconds later a crater erupts in the wind-polished ice-top to the right, showering us with frozen shrapnel. We swerve again, closing now, and another crater bursts open to our right. Chaingun fire peppers us and I feel two of us are hit, one in the thigh, one in the chest.

"Bastards," Ferrily grunts.

"Hold fast," I call. "We're on them in seconds. Ferrily take your team left up the southern stairwell, Tigrates take yours up through the underbelly, I'll cut a diversionary swathe."

"Aye aye," Tigrates says, "bring it on."

The propellant fades out as we skid into the mine's shadow, unhooking in seconds to form into two teams that race across the sleeting ice. We are the first of all the lowboat teams to arrive. I charge a path direct to the middle, reaching out through the bonds to divert the aim of snipers training in on my chord. Their bullets zip through the air as near misses, burying their hot metal bodies with hissing sighs in the crunchy surface snow.

I hit an ice-draped ladder and climb, monitoring the progress of my two teams. They're in on the bottom floors and clearing corridors already, shooting the life out of backstabbing proto-Rusk and Aleuts, clearly all gathered here in a combination plot to bring us down.

I don't care about their machinations. I only care about my chord and ending this. Up the ladder I fold myself into the building's superstructure, Kaos rifle deployed. I run along a narrow rig corridor, shoot a marine emerging out of cover and roll carefully around the body. I hear the ruckus caused by my teams below and bless them for drawing fire.

I take a shot in the shoulder when I emerge onto command level, but shoot my attacker, an officer, in the heart by way of reply.

He drops with a groan.

In the distance more rockets blast, jolting the gantry floor. Gunfire echoes scatter up exposed outer corridors like scree pebbles tossed down a well. I sprint and shoot my way to the mine's apex, dropping marines in the uniforms of two different nations until I blast through a final door into the mine's conning tower.

Two briskly uniformed men stand in a room over a holographic map, the pips on their collars identifying them as generals.

"How?" one of them asks, looking at me in disbelief.

"Time travel, fucker," I say, and shoot them both in the head.

They had planned far worse for me. Of what little mind I had left after riding out their mindbomb in the EMR, they must have taken half. They jacked me nearly as hard as my adoptive parents did, searching for the secret of how I survived. All they left behind was broken memories and regret.

Now there's no regret.

At their control panels I set the mine to overload capacity. It isn't easy but I have the expertise of hackers, engineers and marines all rolled into my Soul Jacker's head still, and I work the command path through the computer's systems like I'm running a Solid Core maze, disabling safeties and churning the drill deeper into the red.

There are hundreds of enemy marines hidden here still. I can feel them spread out through the decks, perhaps enough to turn the tide of the battle now we've used up the element of surprise. Even in the best case victory we'd still lose dozens more digging them out of their bunkers like the brood from their Courts, and I won't stand for a single death more.

I shoot the display to disable it then call through the HUD. "All teams out on the ice, explosion in T-minus five, the whole thing's going to blow."

"Affirmed," Tigrates and Ferrily come back.

I leap on an ice-line from the top-floor gantry, rappel down at a sprint then run out across the glacier top. After four minutes forty I spin around, encircled by the red blips of my chord on the HUD, to watch the mine erupt. It shoots a year's worth of partially refined hydrates into the sky like a volcano. Boom. The ice melts faster. Everything is as it always should have been.

ME

19. TOWER

This is where I'll make my stand.

The engram mixture takes two days and a night to refine, working with the insufficient equipment in the tanker's Soul-jack lab. It's nothing compared to the gear Ritry Goligh had access to in Calico, not even as well-stocked as his jack-site on the Skulk in proto-Calico.

Lucky then the process is mostly one of subtraction.

I begin with a silver ammonite solution, still the most neutral carrier for engrams, using the whole stock this shabby jack facility has, siphoned out of a battered metal canister long past its use-by-date. I run the fluid through a purification distillation, using flasks, beakers and titration condensers gathered from crew quarters, where they were stowed between batches of mixing up their own version of CSF-vodka.

Heclan and I weren't the last to run a Soul Jacker's still, it seems.

The laboratory gear reminds me of the brood's experimentation with tortured Souls. I sit with the burners running and watch the purified fluid drip through the equipment, thinking about blood and matter and thought.

I seal the refined silvery mixture in an outsized ampoule, with an atmosphere-proof rubber nipple through which I can syringe out the fluid, and a contactless magnetic plate through which the engram data can be copied in. Then begins the harder process of reduction.

The EMR is slipshod and rusted, it barely-

thump thumps

-on command, but I crack open the circuitry and massage the flow of magnetism and electrons with a few simple hacks, cutting out the safety boards and cannibalizing them for parts, soldering in workarounds where I can.

Soul Killer

I lie in the machine and set it to a full Soul download. It scans me and sucks out a facsimile of my Soul, filling up half a solid-state data bank with all the data of my personality; my memories of the chord and the foggy recollections I carry over from Ritry Goligh.

I roll out of the EMR and sit at the seat that would have been Heclan's or Carrolla's, and the longest slog begins. This was Ritry Goligh's specialism, and I only dimly remember it through the communal chord memory. I am more familiar with the bonds and the aether, but they are closed to me now. Physically resonating equipment and magnetically imbued silver are the only way I can reach out into the world. It feels like a hundred-fold deceleration, but at the same time there is a workmanlike pleasure in doing it.

As I isolate and prune memory streams in the copy of my Soul, I feel a powerful affinity for this older, slower way of doing things; molding the shape of the engram like wet clay, slice-by-slice erasing my own mind and leaving only a few load-bearing pillars of memory to sustain a core motivation. It offers up a kind of fulfillment and meaning of its own.

Crafting new Souls. If this isn't godhood I don't know what is.

Soon I bring the first of them in, a woman. I remember her as one of the prostitutes on the Skulk; she has red hair, brown eyes, and I find tears trickle down my cheeks as I look into her vacant pupils. I have destroyed her.

I push the syringe in past her bright white eyeball and inject the engram into her brain. Her Molten Core reacts, and I jack in to massage the Lag away like a kelp-tilling shark, helping the engram to bed in and take root.

Then I bring in the next.

It gets easier with each one that follows, until all forty of my stolen hands lie on the floor around me, ammunition ready to be fired off.

I stand in the monastery cloister with the cave-creature lying slack by my feet, watching as my tanker trawls away, black smoke belching up from its three central funnels. I keep watching until it dissipates across the horizon; forty seeds sent onto the wind in search of the remant survivors of the brood-King's brood. If I can know him as they know him, then perhaps I can defeat him.

In the tower classroom I switch on my communications array. Scavenged from the ship, the electronics are ancient but they can still sync into the last few satellites in the sky and suck down any messages that come from my expanded chord.

Their messages will be my bonds. I have three screens powered by the cave-creature's generators, burning on hydrates; the bones of long-dead dinosaurs. So are we all layers upon layers, feeding on the past. I luxuriate in the buzzing electric smell from my Arctic past, reminding me of raids I fought on and raids I dreamed of in other marines' minds. A glass of Arcloberry gin would be good now.

I chuckle. Carrolla would laugh if he saw me sitting in this place with this drooling man at my feet.

"What the hell is that, some kind of pet?" he'd ask. It would be a joke, but it would horrify him if he really knew.

I climb to the tower's roof, a far higher point than the rollercoaster atop Candyland. From here I can see in every direction; back along this rocky promontory wormed with holes like Lag warrens, forward across the Black Sea, up into the sky. I know what I have to do. It is what Far had us do a long time ago, when there was no other hope.

It will be the deepest jack I've ever done. For that I need the tallest tower I ever built.

Several pallets full of bricks are here, brought up my hands. The mortar is here, the cement mixer is here and a space has been swept clear of old moss.

So I begin.

The cave-creature helps me. This fallen man of the brood works by my side, silent and slobbering. Together we lay down a wide base of bricks around the crown of the tower, building atop its walls as foundation. I peek into his Sunken World and see he's driven by the same old desire to hide himself away.

"It'll be a doorway," I tell him. "A bridge. Not a hiding place."

He doesn't hear me. He puts his bricks atop my bricks and together we raise this thing. There are no memories to sow into the walls, no plaster dust, no hidden ropes to collapse the structure behind us, but I don't need that now. I just need a pillar tall enough to   reach   up   and   touch   the   face   of   god.

20. THE BLOODY BOY

Five days in, god reaches down and touches me.

It is a jolt more total than the shockwave of someone crossing the bridge. I am scarcely attuned to those any more, they've become so commonplace in the last few days. Rather this feels like the deep raw strings of the universe being plucked, like the aether itself has been restructured. I feel it in my mind the same way a mother's pulse vibrates through a forming embryo, beginning to reshape physical matter.

It must be the brood-King forcing his way closer to the inner bridge. The thinning in the air is stronger now, siphoning weight from everything. Perhaps he too is building a tower, using all the world's strength to raise it. So the world feels less dense even here inside my EMR Wall, cast by this helmet I have to wear everywhere I go. I can feel the world turning translucent, as if I could reach out a hand and rub it away like papery old skin, leaving...

I don't know what will be left behind. A blank canvas, perhaps.

The first two floors of my tower are complete. Inside I survey the wooden steps circling upward in a tight spiral; I climb them and look out from the top. The view is much the same, but of course it's not about the view. It's about the effort and the focus, about layering and relayering my own bonds in this space until I've forged a missile strong enough to punch through his shield.

That evening the first of my pawns reports back; she's found another of the brood-King's peer group, a woman. Like my cave-creature, she has Lagged herself with a flood of nonsense engrams then somehow immured herself within a ruined lowboat from a failed subglacic assault launch, lying at the bottom of a shallow ocean basin off the corner of Europe.

My pawn cracked her open and dredged out what flotsam memories she still held of the brood-King, then coded those memories into data transmitted by the satellite link. I transfer them into silver engrams and inject them into myself.

They surge through my Molten Core like incoming Dactyls.

Sitting in the classroom again, I see the boy is clean of blood now, though scars mar his pale flesh, covering every inch of him. They are human bite-marks and rake-marks from sharp nails. One of his ears is mostly missing; a patch of hair on the back his head has been torn away. Two of his fingers are gone at the knuckles, and many of his toes are missing too, giving him an awkward gait.

Still his eyes burn when I dare look into them. Over our lunch one day, I watch as he kills another boy who made a comment about his missing ear.

"You look like a ragged tom-cat," he said, or something similar.

The boy made his intestines erupt outward, just like the girl, though this time not through his mouth.

Another memory crystallizes.

It is an additional viewpoint on the moment we all self-syringed, flushing our minds with the bloody boy closing in. As I push the plunger, I feel the sense that perhaps he is watching, and knows we are doing this. Perhaps he wants us to do this to ourselves, just as he whipped us into line as a boy.

He set an example once, twice, and let the rest of us learn. This self-destruction serves his purposes as much as any; yet it is too late then to undo the suicide I have committed by nonsense engram.

I blink up out of the memory, waiting as the sloshing of the engrams settles in my head. The bloody boy, or the brood-King, is plainly an efficient leader who understands human nature like few others, guiding Souls down the paths he provides for them. He has the wisdom to use fear as both lash and leash, controlling his peers with the least effort possible. I cannot help but admire that.

He is also colossally arrogant. He believed a simple self-syringing would be enough to still these brood members, to hide them away from me, believing I was truly dead. That arrogance may afford me a crack in his shield.

I go to work on the tower with a vengeance while the world continues to thin. I draw my patterns in the air, swirled now with my memory of the brood-King as a boy. Over days more of my pawns report in, telling fragmented tales of the bloody boy drawn from his mad peers; of power and sudden brutality, of his deep focus and ruthless efficiency.

I see that efficiency in the death of the world. There is so little of it left now. I lift my hand before my eyes and it is gossamer thin, glowing through with the setting sun. T-minus two days, I think, as the latest pluck through the aether almost pulls a piece of my fragile Soul away. Under such a draw, I wonder if Loralena and my children are even still alive.

I stop eating and sleeping and put all my remaining hours and energy into the tower. It doesn't matter if I die. This body is nothing to me anyway. The tower climbs until the morning of the last day, T-minus zero, when at last I mortar on the last brick. The last of my pawns report in through air barely thick enough to carry the message, and I make their findings part of myself. Perhaps this knowledge will be enough to insert me like a key into the lock of the boy's golden shield. I climb to the top of my tower with fresh memories in my mind and look out over the dawn sky.

Know thy enemy.

Everything is to play for now. My cave creature is dead below, collapsed by the suck of the brood-King. The world is dying around me. I can barely see the sunrise, diaphanous against the bleached-white sky. He is going to remake us all. His next tsunami pull is coming even now, and I am ready for it.

Fuck the brood-King. I am Me, one seventh of Ritry Goligh, and you do not get to become a god on my watch. I throw my EMR helmet down into the water below, place my hands on the walls of my tower and throw my mind open to the bonds.

The brood-King rushes in like a tsunami.

--.

P. RUIN

I know Ven is waiting for me on the subglacic with manacles and pistol at ready. I can feel it, as I stand with my marines by the huge crater of melted ice where the mine once churned and burned. The edges of the ice have run smooth and blue with the melt, like a waterslide in Candyland.

Flashes of a different past, or future, bounce in my head like bondless gold atoms.

"Good job, Rit," Ferrily says. She smacks me on the butt. "You should come fight more often. I don't know who put you in charge but you pulled it off."

"I put myself in charge," I say to her. Her helmet's off now that the blizzard has died down, showing her blonde hair braided tightly to her skull.

Tigrates comes over, her helmet off as well. She looks almost identical to Ferrily, another blonde with her hair in tight rows, bulkier than I am and built for war. They could almost be twins. I recognize La and Ti in them, my own crew.

Ferrily laughs. "Put yourself in charge? Well all hail that. I guess fucking the boss comes with benefits."

Tigrates laughs and punches me in the shoulder.

I look back at the subglacic, far below and barely emerging through the water, its periscope a dark fin through chunks of ice, and understand that I can't go back. The War is over for me now. I can't bear to Lag Ven again, but if I go back I'll have to, because all she wants is to capture or kill me; I can feel her rage from here. I'd have to erase huge chunks of her mind on top of the massive damage I've already done. My manipulation has colored every memory she has of me, and I can't fix that. Even if I tried, she'd be a completely different person when I was done.

I should have thought about this more. At least she's alive.

"She didn't approve it," I say.

"What?" Ferrily asks.

I look at her. So this is how it goes. "She didn't approve it," I repeat, "she thinks I'm a traitor and I was trying to sabotage us all."

Ferrily's face wrinkles, trying to discern where the joke is in what I just said. I make it simple and Lag her. I Lag Tigrates. I make it so they haven't seen me since the raid. I Lag the minds of my other marines, leaving the same simple memory:

I died in the explosion.

I turn away and walk into the white.

For an hour I trudge through snow. Steadily the power in my suit wears down and the cold creeps in. I'm waiting, but there is no apotheosis, no sign of Solfeje, and no answers emerge. In the mindless white, I wonder if I've passed some kind of trial or failed it, or if there was never any chance at apotheosis and this is just reality. I keep walking but nothing changes.

I sit down on a low crag in the ice to wait, and a blizzard folds around me. I wait a long time and think a lot of long, slow thoughts.

I have still lost Ven. She may not be dead but she will never be mine again. Heclan and the others are still alive, but I can never go back to them. I am dead in their world. I am a hero now, or a traitor, but not the Ritry Goligh they knew.

It gets colder as the suit power drains. I try to decide if any of this is matters. What would happen if I die here? What change have I really made?

My suit beeps a warning.

10%

I could sit here and the dying would come easily. Would this be letting them all down, I wonder, or is an embrace of death the thing required to get back to the Hollow Star? I wonder if Solfeje has made a better job of it than me. I don't know any more if I care.

I've made so many mistakes.

I think of Loralena. I remember her first painting of me, the one she never showed, that showed Ritry Goligh's mind in beautiful, loving detail. All the tones of the chord were in it, as seamless together as any mother's pulse. In that she painted me too, Me as one tone in the chord, and it is that union which I think Loralena saw when she first met Ritry Goligh. Though he was always alone, he was also always a tribe of many, with me included. Maybe it's what she loved about him. When he married her and bore children with her we all became a part of each others' tribes.

She's my sister now. She's my wife. I owe it to her and the rest of the chord to get up and keep going. If death is the way out, it will still be waiting when I die.

I stand and head for a blip on my HUD radar. With the last of the juice in my suit I hit upon a privateer mine. It is a small iron-pylon structure, bolted to the ice and drilled diagonally into the hydrate bed at the edge of the proto-Rusk rig. The crew is five-strong, shuttered in tight after the blizzard, and they are no match for me through the bonds.

I take them and their little ship, an altered lowboat, and together we run away.

Q. PROTO-CALICO

I wash up on the Skulk-shores of proto-Calico, Lagging my new crew and sending them on their way. For all I've changed things, things haven't changed here at all. Walking up the swarming night-alley of skulk 47 I hear news of the neo-Armorican victory on the air, foiling an ambush plot. All around are drunken freighters, frazzled whores and crusty AWOL marines like me, little more than boys and girls running underfoot smoking haze and swigging CSF-booze.

This is the world I was born into. It's all fucked; everyone looking out for themselves. No one cares about these lost marines, no one cares about these whores, no one cares about the lost.

My jack-site alley is much the same; lined with broken buildings made from salvaged dreams, though it's more sparse than I remember because of course this is earlier than I was ever here, and they're still rebuilding after the last tsunami.

I go to the blue-tarp park and sit. I see the homeless man sitting across from me, an ex-marine washed out of the service early. It's years earlier than the original Ritry Goligh came here, after global accords forced the proto-Rusk to release him. He came and found this guy was already here. Perhaps he's even more lost than me.

I nod at him. He nods at me and holds out a clear bottle of liquor, like we're already old friends. Somehow he knows what I am. By his side are the low smoldering coals of a newsprint-roasted crull, and I feel caught between times. Ven and my crew are just as lost to me as they were to the original Ritry, so there's nothing here left for me. I get up and go over to the marine, take the bottle and swig it down.

"What happened to you, Ritry?"

I wake in a dim and rocking space of rotting wood and salt, lying on the floor; probably one of the abandoned fishing ships moored off the Skulks. I must have crawled here for shelter, too drunk to think. The hull creaks as the ocean laps it against the Skulk flotation barrels.

I roll and see there's a man sitting on a chair nearby, illuminated by the faint glow of lamplight. I laugh out loud to see him. It comes out as a few spluttered wheezes, which he frowns at.

Mr. Ruin.

He's wearing his gray suit, he's holding his gray cane, but there's no corpse at his feet and no two-cornered hat on his head. Rather he's looking at me with intense curiosity and none of the all-knowing arrogance he had when we first met.

Mr. Ruin. Strangely I feel happy to see him; like the old friend he always wanted us to be. Maybe he alone could understand what I've been through. I feel him probing me through the bonds, searching for answers. He must have noticed my erratic actions: leaving the subglacic in the middle of an engagement, coming here and doing this. All his plans for me are going awry. He gasps as I throw up a Wall on the bonds to block his tampering.

"How did you do that?" he asks, his eyes widening.

I get to my feet and some new understanding floods into my mind. Perhaps this is what I'm meant to do now, to change things in some larger way. I reach out to the bonds and see that I was always stronger than him, I just didn't know it. His eyes go wider still as I freeze him in place with the Lag.

"You want to be my friend, don't you?" I ask, pushing my hangover aside. "Mr. Ruin, you call yourself. You want to know what it feels like to belong, to be so close to someone again like you were with Napoleon, and you've chosen me. You've been watching me since before I was birthed from my artificial womb, watching and waiting for the right moment to strike, is that about right?"

It looks like his eyes are going to burst out with shock. For all my life he's been a cat toying with a mouse, biding his time. He was so patient. Now the mouse has become the cat, and he's my prey. He tries to speak but I squeeze his voice box closed.

"You get what you always wanted, Ruin. I'm here. You're here. Let's do something amazing together. Do you remember the Suns?"

His jaw drops.

"That's right, your lord and master. We're going to kill him. And do you know his greatest general, the boy covered in blood?"

If I wasn't holding him up I think he'd probably faint about now.

"We're going to kill him too."

ME

21. MAKE ME PROUD

I race the King to the bridge in my Solid Core, punching through the locks Far placed on my blast door to burst out into the aether, where everything has changed. I stare in horror; where once there were billions of Soul-stars like endless pinholes of light poked through a velvet black canopy, now it is nearly all darkness.

The lights are winking out and all around me is the brood-King. The bloody boy. I feel him like dark matter in the aether, draining all Souls into himself. He hangs in the center as a massive red star, his golden shield billowing in space where King Ruin's twin red suns once revolved, shining like the end of the world.

I soar out to meet him.

RITY GOLIGH

His voice rings within me, stripping at the strength I've mustered like lava burning away the Bathyscaphe's protective brick layers. There is no surprise in his flat tone, no anger that I am still alive, rather there is a sense of welcoming.

YOU HAVE COME IN TIME TO WITNESS THE BEGINNING

I jack harder still, streaming through the empty darkness where stars once hung. I have no time to look for Loralena, for Art and Mem; I can only hope they are still here somewhere as all the Souls die.

I AM GLAD TO SEE YOU AGAIN. IT SHOULD BE YOU AND I AT THE END

I stream through the aether toward his red dwarf Soul, cast now with a rippling reflection of his face; massive and covered in old scars, battle-worn and insurgent and unstoppable. One of his spears spikes toward me and cuts through all of my defenses with ease, puncturing my middle. I snap it off and rush on, so close to his golden shield now that his face warps like the thumping electrostatic of a guttering EMR.

I AM SO GLAD TO SEE YOU

He says it even as he tries to kill me.

I thrust and arc through the airless aether, propelled by the tower and a lifetime of roots left behind. More of his spears shoot through me but I drive into the pain, because this is my aether and he has no right to steal it like this.

YOU AND I AT THE END, VICTIMS BOTH

His golden shield flickers before me, solidifying at my approach but still translucent, and I peer through to a scene below. There is a vast trebuchet on the surface of his red star, its one massive wooden arm groaning beneath all the stolen weight of the aether. At the other end of the arm sits the bloody boy, ready to bring on the end.

The blood is fresh upon his face still, slicking down from his mouth. There are bite wounds covering every part of him. I see it and even as I see it, the voice knows what I know.

YOU SEE ME NOW

I feel the universe of his thoughts encircle me like the fist of his Soul around the girl who vomited her entrails. Before I was a fly at the periphery but now I fall under the full focus of his power.

Four more spears spike through my shoulders and hips and pin me to the aether, but I have pieces of him inside my Soul now and I can't be stopped so easily.

"You and me at the end," I shout as I rush closer, as proximity blows my image massive across the outer skin of his golden shield, and for a moment I feel what Doe must have felt when plunging into the depths of King Ruin to die; these bonds are the strongest, which are given for love. These are the bonds King Ruin could only break once, because all he ever loved was himself. These are the sacrifices I have ridden this far, with all my chord lost just to reach this point.

My reflection warps then pops like a soap bubble as I plunge into the thick of golden shield. Memories spray everywhere like bondless atoms from Doe's shoulder accelerator and I see it all, the boy's story rushing in just as I rush into him, beginning with an:

Soul Killer

Invasion.

Every instant is an invasion of my Soul as they break in again and again, and I can do nothing but take it, my body so small, a year old perhaps, and always there is that-

thump thump, thump thump

-that is not a pulse but the hammering of the machine that clamps me open to let them in. They killed one half of me already and I'm so alone.

Solfeje and Solmiz. We were made for each other, twin pillars of one pulse meant to always be together, and they killed him. His body crumpled under their endless invasions so long ago, he vomited up his innards with the poison they force-fed him, and what could I do?

I tried to hold him in my tiny arms but I couldn't. They pulled the pieces of him apart then used them to jack deeper in, digging until my thoughts bled with a-

THUMP THUMP, THUMP THUMP

-that would forever echo with what I'd lost, each answering beat only an echo of the first, with his tone never sounding again.

There is no place I can escape from their endless experimentation. I become what they want, just crusts of memory laid end over end with the tortured memory of Solmiz written across my spreading infant mind. My brain builds itself out of his loss, so his absence becomes forever a part of my Soul.

I grow and their invasions redouble. They batter at my thoughts, groping for a way through the maze to the center, tearing chunks away in their frenzied search for the bridge. They grind Solmiz's corpse into me like mortar so that every path they stamp is lined with his ash, but still they cannot find the way.

At some point they bring me up to the world.

I am perhaps seven years old by then, lying in a thumping metal tray as pipes pull out from my spine. Through the glare of light I see an endless hall stretching away, and with it come words that I don't yet understand, but will come to.

Court.

This is a Court and I am just another failed experiment.

Liquid drains around me, the thumping sound fades and the glass dome overhead peels back. This machine has cocooned me in an artificial womb all my life. I see others like me sitting up, hundreds of them in their wombs too, all broken and failed.

I can feel their wounded thoughts, each damaged in ways a shade different to me, gradations in a meticulous experimental plan. They too have invaded, and tortured and now we are to fight for the amusement of the master we have failed to please.

MAKE ME PROUD

His voice rings in my mind, a distant presence I have felt all my existence but never truly known, the one who murdered Solmiz and left me alone; my god, my lord and my tormentor.

I understand what must be done.

My body decants to the floor and in seconds I feel pain. It ties me to this weak flesh, but I know this flesh is not what I am. I am only a passenger in an organic machine, the crust they couldn't scrape away, the echo of Solmiz in my dreams, and I live in a place very far from here.

I look down and see the first of my toes disappear. A boy larger than me has bitten it away. Now he lunges, and I have a moment to pity him, because I can see all his weaknesses. He doesn't have the strength that I have, doesn't have it innately, and so he must die.

With my mind I stun him, then pull my bleeding foot from his mouth and stand, ignoring the pain. It does not compare to the pain I have known all my life. It is a relief. I look at the others while he lies on the ground. Already they are fighting and dying. They are larger than me, and stronger, and they are all mine.

I stamp the boy's throat then I fling myself into the fray. Size does not matter here. The strength of their bodies has no impact upon me. What matters is the Soul, and they trained me well for this.

They surge before me and I break them one after another. I squeeze and they burst; from the eyes, from the ears, from the nostrils. Their blood coats my face and I wear it as a mask. Hundreds of them fall one after another as their deaths make me stronger, and throughout I think of Solmiz. Every pulse of my heart is his name, echoing endlessly with absence.

It's wrong that this was done to me. My lord was wrong and this wound can never be right. I enact my rage upon them, and before my rage their Souls vanish. I am too angry to be killed.

Finally there are none left. Hundred of bodies surround me. Blood drips from my hair; the wounds they have inflicted cover this body. I stand and wait for my cruel lord to come.

He comes.

"I am so proud of you," he says.

Days have passed in the slaughter, and I have learned much. I know now that my lord is called the Suns, and this figure is his hand, sent to me as an emissary. I know that I am the victor of a very special Court. I feel pride and disgust.

"There is a school waiting for you," the Suns' hand says. "Come."

I go.

The school is filled with children older than I, and they are soft. I give them examples of my power until the lesson is taught. I give more lessons until it is burned deeply into their Souls. I thought I had come here to learn, but now I see I was brought here to teach; not just these children, but the brood, the world, and even the Suns itself.

My lord should not have killed Solmiz. The world should not have allowed it. So I will teach them all to be better. I will unmake everything they have done and rewrite it afresh.

For Solmiz I will do all this and more.

I break through the shield and gasp for air in an airless space, now face-to-face with the bloody boy within his trebuchet carriage. The great throwing arm creaks with the weight of so many stolen Souls ready to propel us on; the whole life of the aether. He smiles at me, blood leaking from his gums, then holds a knife to his own throat. I remember what Far said about Disjunct, and understand why he never found the path to apotheosis. To reach the inner bridge of the aether you have to sacrifice everything that exists.

"You and me at the end," the boys says, and slits his own throat. Blood sprays out. Before the knife can drop I snatch it and slit my throat too.

The trebuchet fires as we die and the tether keeping this universe alive breaks; the weight of all Souls drops and some dying part of us is flung out and up with all the force of a billion aether-wide Disjuncts. At once we reach incomprehensible speed, faster than Far ever imagined possible; the Bathyscaphe forges around me and another forges around the boy even as the dust of so many burned bonds coalesces around us into the encircling shell of an asteroidal ferryboat.

CHTHONIC ROCK

-comes the voice of the brood-King in my mind, of the bloody boy, and together we hurtle across the vast distances to the inner bridge of the aether, to the blazing purple Hollow Star at the heart of all things, toward a cataclysmic race for godhood that neither of us can escape.

--.

R. ASCENT

For six months we train. I keep a lock on Ruin at all times and I use his Soul like a punching bag. We go together to all the ruins I visited alone some ten years later. The godships are much the same, though there are still a few holdouts living on them at this point, amidst the giant rusted hulls and upturned rooms, running along their chain walkways as I pull up in Don Zachary's speedboat.

Don Zachary is of course a younger man now, but he hardly looks it, already gnarly and twisted. His empire is much the same, but twenty years away from being ready to quakeseed the world. This is an era when the War is just beginning to resolve, and when I go to him to borrow his boat for old time's sake, he's only looking forward to the days of peace to come and the chance to consolidate what he already has.

After sucking strength from the Don and the godships, we go to the shark-fighting arena, and I draw the old violence and loss out of it. We go to the sunken subglacic and I suck out the jealousy of its mad old captain. We go to all the other locations Ruin would write out in his folder for me years later; best of them all is an expired vault buried in a jut of Arctic rock where once all the seeds of humanity were stored, until the tsunamis crashed in and killed the climate-control generators, leaving the seeds to die.

Standing inside it I feel the immense sense of loss, all these patterns gone forever from the aether, and I swallow them down. I do the same in the abandoned Wall train station, and in a military bunker blown into the bedrock of Calico, and wider back along Mr. Ruin's trail hoovering up bonds and strength wherever we go; into the Hollow Desert, across to the fringe wastelands of neo-Armorica, trawling the blasted nuclear craters of Europe.

I practice my jacks on him. I run circles around his frazzled Molten Core, confounding his Lag and causing his Napoleonic plastic soldiers to shoot each other full of holes. At the last we sit on the rollercoaster rails at the top of Candyland with the sweet fog of boiled sweets in the air, and I tell him my whole story.

"I build the tower right here," I tell him. "You never see it coming. I come through the bridge, just enough to erase my family from your mind. I flood your mind here. And over there," I point, "somewhere along the Wall line, the Suns comes for me. I had a hard time with him."

Ruin listens, befuddled. His mind doesn't work so well at the moment, I've turned him around so much. I've taken everything I need though, more than enough to rupture all the golden shells there are. I can bring down King Ruin in minutes. I can bring down the bloody boy.

So I do it.

Into my own mind I go to man the Bathyscaphe alone, surging up through the Molten Core and grapneling into the Solid Core, running the maze in instants and bursting through the aetheric bridge with ease.

The thunderclap of my arrival rings out across the aether and I fly out with it, riding the crest of the boom as fast as memory, to the great red revolving Suns. I break them open with a thought. Their golden shell peels back and I wither those suns to dry black pebbles.

So simple. In my hands the Suns die, and all their countless spider lines out to a thousand Courts around the world die too, releasing tens of thousands from suffering and shearing every brood member away from their lord and father.

I give the bloody boy no chance to respond. I ride the dissolution up to his Soul while he is buried deep in the mind of an experimental victim, still fishing for the route to the aetheric bridge. He's been hunting it all his life. I take hold of his Soul and squeeze.

He squeezes back.

For an impossible moment he looks into my Soul, and sees everything: everything I have done and everything I have changed back through time to the Hollow Star and the Chthonic Rock and beyond. He sees it all before his grip begins to fade, and in the fragment of time before I crush him to nothing, he speaks.

YOU LACK IMAGINATION.

Then he's gone. The brood-King is dead, withered away.

Soul Killer

I rouse in Candyland. Mr. Ruin is sobbing beside me. Everything he knows has just been destroyed.

It's the same for me.

I feel empty inside. I have changed the aether forever; I've killed the King and the brood-King both, but I don't feel any better. I have saved Ven and my old chord, ended the War early and ensuring the survival of tens of thousands, so why do I feel so hollow?

Mr. Ruin's sobs tear at my heart. I have been cruel to him needlessly. I go to Lag him but halt, because that would be for my comfort only, not for his. The pain would remain inside him, festering like a gangrenous wound. I could Lag it wholly away but what would that make me now?

A sob escapes my lips as the emptiness settles in; a void I couldn't see before with the mission to kill the Kings looming so large. Now it is clear; I have lost everything I thought I might gain. Ven and my subglacic chord are dead to me; the first woman I ever loved and the first family I ever had, and now I've set myself on a path that will not be the same as my old one.

The truth hits me like an ideation grenade; I have lost Loralena.

There is no way the man I am now will form the exact same union with her as before, and without that my children Art and Mem will never be born. Maybe she would still love me and maybe we would still have children, but they will not be the same.

They are gone.

I drop to my knees beside Mr. Ruin, scarcely able to breathe. I have done this to myself. Is it real? Have I really done these things?

The brood-King's last words echo in my mind.

YOU LACK IMAGINATION

I feel sick with it.

I look back on everything I have done in my pursuit of Solfeje, or godhood, or my own happiness. Even these meager dreams have ruined me. How could I become a god, and take charge of all Souls at once, when I cannot even control my own?

How could I deserve apotheosis?

I look at Mr. Ruin and tears stream down my cheeks. I have failed in spite of all my efforts, and I don't know what to do. Perhaps the bloody boy has won. I throw my head back and scream into the sky.

"Solfeje!" It seems to be the only word and only name that matters now. With the emptiness comes understanding, like a curse; I know who she is and what she represents. I understand things I never glimpsed before; how much stronger than me she is. Her suffering was greater. Her dedication was brighter. Maybe she knows the way.

"Solfeje!"

The world cracks under the force of my will and I lean into it, crowbarring the aether open with my Soul. The rollercoaster underfoot bends out of existence, Calico peels back like a chrysalis skin to be replaced by pulsing purple sands and fizzing white skies. Mr. Ruin and the sea and the Wall all disappear, and I'm left standing atop the smoking, crater-pocked wreck of the Bathyscaphe. The brick cladding is ruptured, the metal crumpled and it rests nose-down and half-buried in glinting purple sand near the peak of an immense mountain. I look out over a windswept purple desert spotted with wrecked ships and buried buildings. I think I can make out badly-drawn facsimiles of the godship cluster, and my lost arene tank, and the hydrate rig I blew up in the Arctic.

I stare with tears drying on my cheeks. In the black heavens the orbital ring of Chthonic Rocks hangs like a line of pebbles glimpsed through shallow water. Ahead of me rises the apex of the mountain, crested with a point of impossible bright, pulsing purple light.

The Hollow Star. The inner bridge of the aether. I understand it all.

"I killed you."

I turn to see Solfeje standing on the slope a short way distant. Solfeje, this pulse of the bloody boy. She looks far more powerful than I feel; armored in certainty shines, wielding rage as a weapon I've already lost. Her icy eyes are resolute, while I feel weaker than ever. The things I have done have taken a toll on me, though I was never as strong as her.

A silent moment passes between us. No wind rustles the sands of the Hollow Star. Nothing moves or breathes in this place, so near the summit, and I see it all. A hope, perhaps, tumbling back to the mission pack that began this all: a piece of paper with an arch and simple labels.

YOU

ME

"We are the pillars," I say. My voice rings out like a message on blood-mic, carrying a message I'm just beginning to grasp. "You and I."

"It can only be one of us," she says.

But she's wrong.

I know so much more than her now, after living out the dreams I've clung onto for so long, after holding her Soul in my hands and crushing it. I see what she wants and why, and I begin to understand what that means. Where my small alterations led only to greater pain, the tsunami flood of change she brings will undo us all.

So the mission pack was wrong. We are not the pillars; there is no place in the center where we can meet to build an arch, no balance to be found here. I cannot and will not allow either of us to become a god and destroy what so many Souls across the aether have built.

"I'm going to kill you," I tell her.

"You will try," she says, and starts to run. I run too. We reach the bristling light at the Star's apex at the same moment and...

S. NOT THIS

The Hollow Star swallows us up and spits us out.

I tumble and stand; it is a Court, except it is no Court that ever existed. Larger and brighter and unending in scale, it is like the aether itself. In part it looks like the experimental arena where the bloody boy proved himself, but that is far from its entirety, and I can feel countless realities shimmering underneath the surface, just like the ferrywoman's periscope.

At once I'm on the Skulks, standing in the jack-site with Mei-An on the EMR tray before me, but I'm also atop the rails in Candyland with Mr. Ruin begging me to stop, and I'm in the seafort where Harim Ongshoy fought to his miserable death, and I'm in the Sunken World slogging through mud with the chord, and I'm in the monastery with the bloody boy teaching his lessons to the brood, and I'm in the godships, and on the Chthonic Rock, and Loralena is alive then she's dead, and Ven is dead then she's alive, and what is it all for?

I gasp, dizzy from the motionless revolutions. So many possibilities spin beneath my feet, and I see that this is all the power of a god.

I blink.

In the middle of the non-Court hangs King Ruin; one twin alive, one dead. Conjoined, they are a horror. One withered, one glaring, while all around us another experimental brood are killing each other like they've done so many times before; raking with cracked nails, biting with chipped teeth.

In their midst stands the bloody boy. Solfeje. She is alone but not alone, for every child fighting in this Court here carries the same face; a face I recognize from her Soul.

Solmiz. The dead half of her pulse.

"He didn't die on the sublavic," I say.

Solfeje looks at me with something like pity. I am so slow to understand. "He was always dead, Me. I had him for moments only before the Suns gouged him away."

I look at these child copies of Solmiz, every one bloodied and staring at me now. I can hardly conceive of losing this much. My adoptive parents jacked into my mind but they didn't kill the chord. I kept seven parts of myself alive, while Solfeje lost fully half of who she was.

"You've suffered," I say. It is empty to say this really, because she knows. We both know; have been in and out of each other's mind for a lifetime, it feels. I know her, I know him, and she knows me.

"You suffered as well," she says. "You led the way. And you would never have helped me."

There is nothing to say to this, no answer to give. She's right.

"So we fight," I say.

Now she smiles; it is sad with the weight of my lost potential. "There will be no fight. Your chord are dead, Ritry Goligh. I can feel the defeat radiating off you. You are weak and lost, while I have all the strength of the world and a purpose to fulfill."

I can't argue. Her will is bright and swollen with all the Souls of the aether. "Stolen strength."

Her smile turns to pity. "Of course it is stolen, as you stole every shred you ever took. How else could you beat Mr. Ruin, how else could you bring down the Suns and cross the aetheric bridge so many times? You stole from the world too. It's only I who would repair the damage we've all done. Only I want to make it better."

I know what she wants now. It will be an end to us all; a hollowing out with consequences that last forever. "With a flood."

"With a new creation! I will remake it better, Me. Do you honestly believe your petty ambitions compare to mine? You've known love, you've had companions, but does any of that make what King Ruin did to you worthwhile? Does any of that compensate for what your parents did?"

I look at her and see her compassion thrusting with the weight of a tsunami, ready to crush all in its path.

"It's too much, Solfeje. To end the world for your suffering? You can't make this choice for everyone."

She takes a step toward me. "I'm the only one who can. The aether will be kinder. Who else can offer that?"

I shake my head. I see new things now, the patterns in the flow of bonds all building toward something so beautiful. I tampered with those flows at the smallest scale, and still I poisoned them all. "You'll undo everything we've learned. With every loss, every love, every drop of suffering and slice of joy the aether's been learning, Solfeje. It's grown rich and vibrant, and I know you see this too. Our past pains as well as our joys inform every new Soul that is born. How could it be any other way? We're getting better, Solfeje. The aether is learning through us. Have faith in that."

Her sad smile fades. "Three thousand years ago there were massacres, Me. Today there are massacres. The only difference is scale. The aether is broken and a revolution is needed. We come from a world where all of us are victims, of each other, of circumstance, of those that came before and those that come after us. We are all prey in our time, even King Ruin. Nobody dies happy in their bed, satisfied with their life. For us all life is cruel and brutal and solitary, and I won't accept it any more, Me. Now take your shot. Anything you do, I will undo. I know you see that. Look at my army. You've come here as a token, so make your token gesture."

I look at her and see a lifetime of loneliness even deeper than Mr. Ruin's, with no single moment of respite. There was no sense of belonging for her; no Ven, no Heclan, no Loralena or Carrolla. She had only herself and the King. There was never anything worth living for but Solmiz, whose ground-down corpse she has carried with her ever since his death, a constant reminder of what she could never have.

Her life has been cruel, and I don't know how to argue with her. I don't know if I can even understand what she's lost. I have lost Doe and Ray and Far and the others, but I had them for so long. We were together for years. But if I'd never had them at all?

The abyss that would open is terrifying; to be so completely alone in a world. Perhaps I'd be just like her.

But I'm not like her. The aether admitted us both to this place, and maybe we will be twin pillars of the same world, if I can just find a way to build that final arching bridge between us.

"Look wider, Solfeje," I say. "Look at so many others who've lived well, who've loved, who've found belonging and added happiness to the world. You can't judge all of them. The wonders they brought have buoyed us all."

"It's not enough."

"It has to be! The world can also be kind, Solfeje. Don't let your anger blind you to the truth."

Her eyes blaze with passion. "And am I angry, Me? Do you see anger in me?"

I did. As a boy it was all she knew, but not now. Now I just see this perversion of love, this drive to protect us all by filing off every sharp edge and taking away any hurt so we can start over anew.

"It isn't anger," I say, "it's surrender. How will you remake us, like seaweed growing in sludge with enough sunlight for all? There will be no struggle, no growth, no betterment. How can that be better? Suffering is the road we have to walk."

"Massacres, Me. Cruelty. Seaweed would be better."

I look into her eyes and see they are set as though carved out of stone. She has become her pillar as I have become mine, built on a lifetime of choices and leading to this moment. I don't see any place where an arch could join us together, and I don't know how to defeat her.

"You can't, because you lack imagination," she says, smoothly reading my thoughts. "I said it then and I'll say it again. You speak of grand notions, of the glacial love of the far-off aether growing warmer, but it's yourself you're fighting for, the ties binding you alone. I only need say their names and you'll fall to your knees begging me to spare them. Ven, Art, Yena, Ray, and so on." She points her finger at me. "I watched how you spent your second chance, Me. You're here for the ones who loved you and you alone. You're not fighting for grand ideals but for the tiny corner of comfort you've carved out for yourself. What does that mean to me or anyone? It's nothing. It's selfishness wrapped up in a self-righteous flag, and that's all."

I can only nod along now, because she's right. A self-righteous flag. My own tiny corner of comfort. It's why I'm here, because I am selfish and I am fighting for myself. This is what I saw in my past. I saved Ven and the crew by destroying the hydrate mine, killing hundreds of others to save her and change the course of history, but by what right did I do it, and for whose benefit?

I did it for myself.

That realization hollows me out afresh. I must be more than just this rush to get enough love for myself, but what more am I? What about selflessness and sacrifice? What about real love given for nothing? What about the homeless man who shared his liquor with me on the Skulk, and showed me his family in the tent, and helped me find a way forward?

I have to be more, so I make the choice to become more. I am on the verge of godhood now, after all, and so I must act and think like a god. This is about the Souls of us all, and her words echo in my mind.

YOU LACK IMAGINATION.

It too is my fault. I can't let it be my fault any more.

"It's a mercy I'm bringing," Solfeje says, "the greatest mercy."

But she's wrong, and it falls to me to show her why. With what little strength I have left, I take my shot.

The aether bends. I plunge backward through space and time, through the heart of the Hollow Star all furious and burning and back to the world we've left behind and into the Soul of Solfeje as a helpless child.

Before she was the brood-King, before she became the bloody boy and back to the time when the researchers of her experimental Court were drilling into her again and again, searching for the bridge. She couldn't hide the way I once had, she had no Far to screen her, she could only scream out soundlessly for someone to help, but no help ever came.

So I come.

I do not save her because I can't try to undo the past again. I do not change her life or the path she must take, I merely stand within her while all the worst transgressions are done, and hold her battered Soul with my own and whisper simple words into her Solid Core:

not this

I say it as Far once said it for me.

not this

not only this

It does nothing for her. It does everything. She is no longer alone. She has a witness, though she can't understand how or from where. There is someone with her and within her, some being that loves her and tells her she deserves better and this is not how her life should be.

It changes her. I feel the fabric of her mind shifting the longer I stay, so I stay through it all. With me there watching she has someone to endure for and something to fight towards; she is no longer a victim, instead she becomes a survivor.

I am there as she kills the children in the Court, and I am there as she teaches her lessons in the King's school. I am there through every atrocity she commits all the way up to now, standing across the Hollow Star from me and staring back.

Tears well in her eyes.

"No," she says.

She sees what I've done. She feels it, she's lived it and now she is changed. This will be my sacrifice, giving all I have to help heal the wound in her Soul. I cross the nothing space of the Court and put my hands on her arms and look into her eyes.

"You were never alone," I say. "You were never unloved. I was always there."

"No!" she shouts now, and a torrent of power hurtles from her to flood across the aether with the stolen life of so many Souls.

"I'm here," I whisper to her through the maelstrom, understanding that this was always what I had to do. "I was always here. I love you, Solfeje, as I love my chord. We can make this better, sister. We can share this with others, daughter. We can hold them all close, mother mine."

She stares at me and tears roll down her cheeks. Even gods cry. She screams. She vanishes.

T. PILLARS

I feel the first stab of her tsunami like a syringe in the head, but it is not what I thought it would be; not erasure but something different, something building up from the past and growing through my mind like a new memory, becoming part of what I am.

In flickers of new memory I see myself as a boy again, an infant in my EMR tray. My researcher parents are jacking into me once more for their endless experimentation, and all seven parts of my Soul are hiding behind Far's scar tissue wall, begging for it to end.

And she is there. Solfeje stands within me with her hand on my heart just as I did for her, whispering into my Soul.

I'm here

It doesn't take away the pain or the hurt, it doesn't change my parents or my past, but it changes me. I too become a survivor, not a victim. I am witnessed through this, and no longer so hopeless and alone.

The memory blooms deeper and now I'm lying in the blue-tarp park screaming, after Mr. Ruin has taken my children and wife from me, while he rapes and tortures them and I lie here helpless and trapped, and she is there in my Soul still, whispering in my mind.

I'm here

I sob to hear her voice, because even here in this worst moment of my life I am no longer alone. I feel myself changing, the bitterness lightening, the old angers spreading as the hurt is shared.

I'm here

I burst into tears too because I see now the pure beauty of what she is doing and has done, this bloody boy, this greatest of Soul jackers, this ruthless brood-King.

She has given this gift to everyone. Every single Soul from past to present and into the future, using the strength that she stole and now returns back like a gift. She has become the god in the heart of every person that ever lived, keeping them and holding them, being there for them forever.

We will never be alone again.

I drop to my knees, overcome with the vastness of it. She has taken the worst of all suffering on her shoulders to help them bear it. I love her for it. If I could I would pray in her name.

It makes me stronger; strong enough to do one more thing, one final act that will change us all going forward, that will add to the aether's endless calculation and truly make us two opposing pillars of this brave new world.

A final time, I open the bridge.

The inner ways of the aether have been a secret for too long, from too many, but the aether is the heart of us all. With Solfeje in my Soul I'm going to share it with them all.

I stretch myself across the aether, becoming so thin I can't stretch any further, until at some point Far joins me across the Disjunct veil of death and lends his mass to the vast skin I'm building. Ray and So join us too, and La and Ti, until finally Doe comes back from whatever far-off place she has been, and together we link arms around the aether.

We grow to dizzying depths across thought and reality, skimming the surface of life and death, encompassing all of history to offer up my own version of the bloody boy's flood.

It is not for the past, but the future. Solfeje has changed everything we ever did, raising us from prey to something new, raising even the lowliest Soul who was humiliated, tortured and murdered in a Court of King Ruin to something better, raising even the son of Don Zachary who died a meaningless death at Mr. Ruin's hands, making our survival conscious and known and returning our lost dignity.

Now I'm going to take that further still.

I stretch so far that I can scarcely remember what I'm doing, until I only see starlight and the Hollow Star and an endless stream of Chthonic Rocks shooting back and forth from countless firework Disjuncts, carrying Souls of the dead home to their source, carrying new Souls out to be born. I stretch until I become simply a mission, just a burning light in the darkness bringing this gift to us all.

It is the most beautiful thing I have ever conceived.

I stretch until the gossamer sheen of my consciousness bursts and I fall like rain across the aether, working changes that will carry all of us forward. I fall like rain over my wife and my children, on tyrants and madmen alike, on ex-marines and whores, on the loved and the lost and the brood and their prey, changing them all.

I give them the bonds. I give them the bridge. I give to all of them the aether, but what I give them more than anything is each other. They will always have a witness in their Souls, thanks to Solfeje. They will always have each other there too, thanks to me. We are two pillars of this new world, and in this new world no Soul will ever be alone or misunderstood again.

King Ruin believed hell was the needs of other people; now we have shared those needs with everyone, and I believe they will make of that connection something far better, stronger and more beautiful than he envisaged. It is a trial, perhaps, another step in the endless calculations as the aetheric Soul works itself to something bigger, bolder and greater.

Then I am falling and fading, a dying god at his limit, until in the last flickering moments as my consciousness ebbs I see all my beloveds again.

"Come," says Doe, and pulls me in. Ray beams at me with his arms spread wide, tooth-loops glinting, and Ti and La are holding hands, and So is waiting with a smile on her sweet, shy face, with Far in the midst of them grinning like I have never seen before. We are all together again, and we take hands and rejoin as a single whole, Ritry Goligh once more, passing together into the purple light of the Hollow Star at the heart of the aether and beyond...

CODA

Mem woke early, with the trails of a strange dream in her mind.

It was of her father, whom she hadn't seen for so long. Ritry Goligh was missing and nobody knew where he had gone. Mem remembered him as the man who used to tuck her in bed and tell her stories until she fell asleep, who danced with her atop the Candyland rollercoaster; the man who taught her how best to tease her little brother by putting fake spiders in his breakfast cereal, who used to swing her around by the arms like an airplane.

But in the dream he was so much more. In the dream he stood with a team of marines all dressed in black atop a subglacic on a burning lake of lava. They all had names like the tones of a chord; Doe and Ray, Me and Far, So and La and Ti, and they were looking up out of the dream toward her.

Waking from the dream, Mem felt as if she knew them.

She walked from her bedroom to find her mother and her brother standing bleary-eyed in the corridor, and at once understood that they had shared the same dream. The weight of that understanding stretched between them like lines sketched in invisible ink through the air.

And not only here. Mem gasped as she felt these new lines spreading everywhere; outward through the glass of their Calico Reach apartment and spreading for a thousand miles in every direction, linking to every Soul in existence.

I'm here

A new voice sounded within her, which she realized had always been there, holding her and buoying her, telling her she was loved. It meant everyone was loved.

I'm here

Mem's eyes welled with tears. Her mother's and brother's eyes filled with tears. It was nothing new. It had been like this all her life but somehow now it felt different. There was a new kind of hope, and an urgency to that hope that she didn't fully understand.

Things were going to be better. It felt like waking from a long nightmare she didn't even know she'd been having; of a cruel man who beat them and lied and wore her father's face, who did the same cruel things again and again, but now all that was finally over.

The sun peeked out through the gray clouds over the tsunami wall. The rain stopped and somewhere behind them a node began to ring. Mem looked at her mother, whose eyes brimmed with tears. She knew. They all knew, now.

Finally.

"Answer it," Loralena said, "it's for you."

Art ran. Mem followed.

ABOUT THE AUTHOR

Michael John Grist is a British/American writer and ruins photographer who lived in Tokyo, Japan for 11 years, and now lives in London, England.

He writes thrilling science fiction and fantasy novels, and used to explore and photograph abandoned places around the world, such as ruined theme parks, military bases, underground bunkers, and ghost towns. These adventures have drawn millions of visitors to his website michaeljohngrist.com, and often provide inspiration for his fiction.

OTHER WORKS

Last Mayor (complete apocalypse thriller)
1. The Last
2. The Lost
3. The Least
1-3 Box Set 1
4. The Loss
5. The List
6. The Laws
7. The Lash
8. The Lies
9. The Lies

Soul Jacker (complete cyberpunk trilogy)
1. Soul Jacker
2. Soul Breaker
3. Soul Killer

Ignifer Cycle (epic fantasy)
1. The Saint's Rise
2. The Rot's War

Short fiction
Cullsman #9- 9 science fiction stories
Death of East - 9 weird tales

EXTRAS

Thank you for reading Soul Killer!

1. There's a glossary of all terms a few pages on.

2. Not an extra but a small ask – if you could review this book on the shop site where you bought it, that would be deeply appreciated. Reviews mean a lot to me and I read and take on board every one.

Find links at www.michaeljohngrist.com/soul-killer

GLOSSARY

Aether – The space beyond the aetheric bridge, where all souls manifest as star-like lights, and lines representing all connections they've ever made with people or places exist.

Aetheric Bridge – The doorway at the center of the Solid Core, beyond which lies the aether. No-one has ever crossed it until Ritry does so.

Aetheric Soul – Another term to describe the aether, though more specifically it refers to all of the souls in aggregate, not the space, and even to the theorized flame from which souls come and to which they return.

Afri-Jarvanese – A language, part African dialect, part Japanese.

Arcloberry – A berry discovered preserved as a seed, deep within the melting Arctic pack ice.

Arctic War – The resource wars for the hydrates under the Arctic ice, in which nations and nation-states cast aside old alliances and made every effort to grab as much ocean as possible. Ritry fought in the Arctic War aboard a subglacic, as a marine.

Arene – The name given to marine who fought in the deserts, hunting for the last reserves of petroleum. They fought in suprarene tanks. Arene is Latin for Sand, hence 'arena.'

Asiatic – A term similar to Asian, but different in that 'Asian' refers to sections of the 'old' world, before sea levels rose and tsunamis leveled whole island nations, while 'Asiatic' refers to the countries and peoples of the new map.

Blood-mic – An internal communication system used by the chord, similar to bone micronodes which capture sound as it transmits through the jaw-bone. Blood-mic captures vibration of sound in the blood, much like sound was transferred to the forming Ritry Goligh in his liquid artificial womb, then relays it to the others.

Bonds – The invisible lines created in space by the passage of human beings. Existence creates bonds, as do thought and emotion. These bonds connect the people who made them to the people, places and things they connected to. Strong emotion, powerful thoughts, powerful action, pain, love, all can create exceptionally powerful bonds. Cutting them, or Lagging them, can create vast power, which can be channeled to exert control over others. They can also be 'surfed,' where their power is used without Lagging, as Ritry does at the godships. These are the resource Mr. Ruin lives off.

Calico – The city Ritry lives outside of, surrounded by a tall tsunami wall. Within the walls life is somewhat utopian, with very little crime or poverty.

Calico Reach – The wealthiest, most exclusive part of Calico, in the hills.

Candlebomb – A type of bomb, like C4.

Chord – A team of 7 marines, each with a name that is one note of a seven-tone scale.

Crull – A genetic cross-breed of sea gulls and crows.

CSF – Cerebro-Spinal fluid, the natural fluid that the brain sits within. Deplete this, for example by drinking a lot of alcohol, and you get a bad headache.

Elba – The island to which Napoleon was banished.

EMR machine – ElectroMagnetic Resonance machine, used by graysmiths to aid in jacking minds. Currently such machines exist as fMRI (functional Magnetic Resonance Imagers) and can be used to take pictures of the brain at work. They don't yet allow writng/rewriting of the mind.

Exos – External suit muscles that augment human power.

Godship – A ship commissioned and boarded during the period of global tsunami while the Arctic War played out, filled with the world's greatest believers. They were all crushed in the tsunami.

Grapnels – Grapnel hooks fired from rifles, with an incoiling function built in.

Soul Jacker – A specialist, like Ritry, who is capable of hacking into another person's mind, and implanting or erasing memories and knowledge. In the Arctic War they served as interrogators, morale officers, briefing and debriefing specialists, skills teachers, and psychologists. Now they primarily work in education, implanting knowledge and massaging it into place. Some, like Ritry, may also erase bad memories. The name comes from the action of extreme forms of hacking, where it seems that the soul itself, or the free will, of a person has been hijacked.

Jack-site – Where a Soul Jacker works, usually equipped with EMR and lots of CSF.

HUD – Heads Up Display, a marine's helmet that can display lots of data on the inner visor-screen.

Engram – What a Soul Jacker injects when imparting new knowledge. It is injected through the eye socket and into the brain as a silvery liquid, containing memories or skills.

Lag, the – The worm-like creature that protects the mind. It seeks to destroy any foreign bodies, including even the inhabitant of that mind, if they come in conscious contact. It can be delayed by giving it thoughts and memories to consume, but it cannot be killed so long as the mind itself is alive.

Lag (v) – Reflecting the erasing action of the Lag, Ritry coins this term to mean erasing memories through the bonds, without resorting to erasing them while jacking in EMR.

Mindbomb – A bomb that functions like an EMP (Electro Magnetic Pulse) for the human mind, stopping all thought and killing any people within range instantly. Soundless and without percussive blast. It can be survived if the mind is shielded within an EMR of some kind.

Molten Core – The exterior part of the brain, most closely related to the gray part, ie the cortex. Embodied during a jack as liquid magma, because it is always in flux.

New Anglais – A new language, a mixture of English and French.

Proto-Calico – The floating raft city that hugs the tsunami wall of Calico, built out of the wreckage of past cities, ships, and anything else. Held up on floating blue barrels, and made up of numerous individual rafts called Skulks. The people who live here have no protection from future tsunami. Their city is essentially ungoverned and lawless, bar the efforts made by Don Zachary to cement his stranglehold over commerce.

QC – Quantum Confusion particles, capable of dissolving regular matter. In this they act a lot like anti-matter, but can be targeted. A QC pistol contains and shoots them.

Rusk, proto-Rusk – Nation-state comprised of remnants of Russian peoples.

Screw, the – The propulsive screw that drives the sublavic ship.

Sino-Rusk – Nation state comprised of partly Russian and partly Chinese nationalities.

Shock-jacks – Stimulants that are stored in sublavic suits, and can be drawn on to negate the effects of shock, pain, and trauma.

Skulks, The – The floating neighborhoods that tile the coast of Calico, making up proto-Calico. They are typically built from flotsam and jetsam, float atop blue barrels, and house the poor, indigent, and those unwilling to live within the order of Calico.

Solid Core – The interior part of the brain, hidden inside the cortex, where no one has ever been before. Here the Lag is stronger, the pathways are myriad and labyrinthine, and somewhere in the center the aetheric bridge is fable to sit. Through this doorway, great power rests. Researchers jacked Ritry for much of his childhood, searching for a way in.

Subglacic – A ship that goes under the ice, used broadly in the Arctic War for stealth and hunting out hydrates.

Sublavic – A ship that goes under lava, used by Ritry's chord of marines to travel through the Molten Core.

Suprarene tank – A giant tank used by arenes who fought in the desert during the war.

Tsunami wall – The wall around Calico, protecting it from giant tsunami brought on by the War and global sea-level change.

59758277R00131

Made in the USA
Columbia, SC
07 June 2019